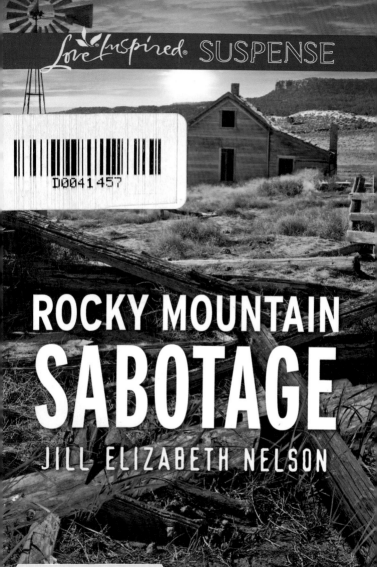

Love Inspired SUSPENSE

D0041457

ROCKY MOUNTAIN
SABOTAGE

JILL ELIZABETH NELSON

LARGER PRINT

Love Inspired SUSPENSE

Suspenseful romances of danger and faith.

AVAILABLE THIS MONTH

ISBN-13: 978-0-373-67828-0
50699

EAN

The fuel was gone. His Challenger 350 had bled out in mere minutes.

He could just barely buy that something might go wrong with one of the engines. But both of them at once? Something was seriously bent about this flight emergency. There was nothing normal about it.

Somehow he had to radio in a mayday. But there was no way he could release the stick with even one hand in order to use the radio. Unless... He glanced sideways at the passenger in the copilot seat. Her torso quivered, and her gaze was fixed straight ahead, but at least she wasn't hysterical.

"Any chance you know how to operate a two-way radio?"

"Y-yes. W-we use one in the hospital for medevac emergencies."

"Put out a distress call. Frequency one-two-one-point-five."

She did as he asked. She performed the mayday drill once...twice...three times. Dead air met every attempt. A spasm visibly gripped her throat. "The radio is dead."

Kent clenched his jaw. "This has to be sabotage, pure and simple," he muttered. But who? Why? Did someone want to kill one of his passengers badly enough to take the life of everyone aboard?

Jill Elizabeth Nelson writes what she likes to read—faith-based tales of adventure seasoned with romance. Parts of the year find her and her husband on the international mission field. Other parts find them at home in rural Minnesota, surrounded by the woods and prairie and four grown children and young grandchildren. More about Jill and her books can be found at jillelizabethnelson.com or Facebook.com/JillElizabethNelson.Author.

Books by Jill Elizabeth Nelson

Love Inspired Suspense

Evidence of Murder
Witness to Murder
Calculated Revenge
Legacy of Lies
Betrayal on the Border
Frame-Up
Shake Down
Rocky Mountain Sabotage

Visit the Author Profile page at Harlequin.com.

ROCKY MOUNTAIN SABOTAGE

JILL ELIZABETH NELSON

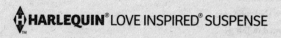

HARLEQUIN® LOVE INSPIRED® SUSPENSE

LOVE INSPIRED BOOKS

Recycling programs for this product may not exist in your area.

ISBN-13: 978-0-373-67828-0

Rocky Mountain Sabotage

Copyright © 2017 by Jill Elizabeth Nelson

www.Harlequin.com

Printed in U.S.A.

A father of the fatherless and a judge for the widows,
is God in His holy habitation.
–Psalms 68:5

For all who suffer the pains of rejection and abandonment.
May you find your healing in the One
who will never leave or forsake you.

ONE

Lauren Carter ground her teeth together as she glared down at rugged Rocky Mountain scenery. Her breath formed patches of milky condensation on the window of the charter jet she'd boarded a little over three hours ago in New York. Thousands of feet below, cloud-wreathed peaks stabbed toward the plane's belly. A little lower, snow-whitened troughs outlined with black ridges resembled an enormous, raggedly striped quilt. Quite breathtaking. She might actually start enjoying this impromptu fall vacation trip to California if not for her mother's annoying question rattling around her brain like a rogue ping-pong ball.

What do you think of our handsome pilot? Why couldn't the two of them have a relaxing getaway—try to rebuild some of the closeness they once shared—without Mom angling to set her up with any male old enough to shave but not yet eligible for a midlife crisis?

Fortunately, that criteria left out the other five passengers on the plane. The executives from three different investment corporations were transportation-pooling to some convention in San Francisco. All of them appeared old enough to be the father Lauren had barely known. One even looked old enough to be her grandfather. And since the copilot, who doubled as cabin attendant, was a female of about Lauren's age of thirty-one, that left Kent Garland on Mother's list—the pilot with sun-streaked brown hair, a chin like one of these rocky ridges, and a gray gaze as cool as one of the snowy peaks. Handsome? Sure, if a woman liked the rugged type.

Something small and hard jabbed Lauren's knee. Mom's fingernail, of course. If she had to lean across the space between their facing seats in order to gain Lauren's attention, the woman was serious about getting an answer.

"Did you hear what I asked, dear?" Mom uttered her words in that quiet, refined-sugar tone she reserved for "discreet" conversation.

Lauren met her mother's stare. "If I had a nickel for every time you've asked something like that, my school loans would be paid off."

Mom's full mouth puckered and long lashes lowered over true-blue eyes, but not in time to disguise irritation. The brightening pink tinge across her mother's high cheekbones betrayed embarrassment at the volume of her daughter's voice. Lauren's face heated as several executives, two seated on the nearby couch and the elder statesman in a leather-bound seat kitty-corner across the aisle, looked up from laptops or Wall Street magazines.

She heaved an internal sigh. *Face it, girl. Your mama is the quintessential Georgia peach, soft and sweet on the outside, but all hard-core on the inside. And you are and always have been a steel safe on the outside and a hot mess on the inside.*

From old photographs and fuzzy, small-child memories, Lauren had long ago become aware that she'd inherited her auburn hair, green eyes, height and build from her AWOL father—which made her something of an Amazon around most other women and many guys. She must have also inherited from him her tendency to erect ironclad walls around her heart. Or maybe that was just how she protected herself from experiencing that kind of abandonment again. At least she wasn't the sort who ran out on family and responsibilities when the going got a little rocky. She assured herself of that fact often, but the balm of self-righteousness did little to soothe the stupid, nagging ache in her core.

Lauren pressed her lips together. You'd think she'd be over her father's desertion by now. Was it something a person could get past? She desperately wanted to feel whole. Even the church-going faith she'd grown up with hadn't yet completely healed the wound.

Mom lowered her head and smoothed an imaginary wrinkle out of her beige pants. A smattering of tiny age spots on the back of her slim hand tattled on her fiftysomething age. "If you'd just let Marlin take care of those loans for you, you'd have a clean slate already. Just the other day, he said to me, 'Nina, talk to that proud girl of yours. I'd like to help her—'"

"We're not going there, either, Mom." Lauren worked at keeping her voice low, but she couldn't hide the ferocity. "He arranged and paid for this plane trip, and I'm grateful, but he's not buying shares in my life. I'm glad you found someone and that you love him, but—"

Her mother's intake of breath and wide gaze shot a pang through Lauren. She cleared her throat. That "oh, honey, you just tracked mud into the house" mannerism worked every time.

"Sorry for snapping at you." Lauren heaved out a breath. "But seriously, the whole idea of this beach getaway is for it to be just you and me—girl time. No husband-hunting."

Mom's gaze returned to hers, a gentle smile flitting across her lips. "I can appreciate that, dear, but what if you happen to run across Mr. Right?"

In spite of herself, Lauren chuckled. Mom was incorrigible. "At this point in my life, I'd have to *run over* Mr. Right in order for him to get my attention. My practice is just getting off the ground. I've got to put in long hours. That's why these few stolen days away with you are so precious to me. I don't want to spend them anywhere but in your company."

Mom beamed at her, and Lauren's heart lightened. Since her mother had married Wall Street mega shark Marlin Barrington two years ago, the closeness she and her mom used to share had all but evaporated. The fact that the guy endorsed his wife's passion for charity work with generous donations should have endeared him with Lauren, but it only made her feel guilty for her resentment of him.

Marlin was the founder and CEO of Peerless One, a billion-dollar investment firm. He schmoozed with movers and shakers all over the planet, and Lauren's elegant mother Nina fit right in. What with participating in charity functions, or hosting gala events at Marlin's

Long Island estate, or appearing on her husband's elbow at Broadway shows or exclusive luncheons, Mom seldom had time for Lauren anymore. Except for this long weekend away that Marlin had facilitated.

She and her mom would have an awesome time pampering themselves at the hotel spa, taking long walks on the beach, enjoying leisurely lunches, shopping at Union Square, exploring Ghirardelli Square and whatever else they felt like doing. No schedule. No expectations. Seriously, after having kept her nose to the grindstone for all these years to become a physician's assistant, she craved a tiny taste of downtime. This trip was going to be okay. Everything was going to be all—

An explosion like the father of all firecrackers sounded somewhere underneath the fuselage, and the plane heaved. If Lauren hadn't been strapped in, her head would have hit the ceiling. The elder executive, who hadn't been wearing his seat belt, was flung forward and landed on all fours with the top of his bushy gray head mashed against the side of her mother's seat. He crouched there, quivering, while Mom squeaked like her windpipe was pinched.

Lauren gazed around as cries of alarm united in an indistinct chorus of questions and exclamations. Thumps toward the back of the plane indicated that others had been thrown from their seats also. Shooting a gaze over her shoulder, she found that one of the passengers lay half way in and half way out of the lavatory, but he was already picking himself up.

She swallowed hard against a suddenly dry throat. What just happened?

The plane lurched again, and from the cockpit area a yelp ended in a heavy thud. Uh-oh, had something happened to one of the pilots? She was facing the cockpit, but she couldn't make out anything from around her mother's seat.

Lauren gripped the arms of her chair as the steady engine rumble morphed into a staccato whine. The cabin began to shake like they were racing over endless speed bumps. The "fasten seat belt" lights blazed red.

Ya think? Lauren's heart hammered as she tightened her own seat belt then checked her mother's. The executive that had been flung out of his seat suddenly lunged upright, shaking his head like a dazed creature.

"Sit down, sir," Lauren called, but the man registered no response to her voice.

Mom's eyes were round as quarters, staring at Lauren. The whites rimmed the blue irises. "God help us." She exhaled a soft moan.

"He will, Mom." Lauren packed all the assurance she could muster into her tone.

Oxygen masks popped down from the ceiling. Her mother grabbed the mask in front of her. As Lauren reached for hers that grandfather-aged executive staggered up the aisle in a direction away from his seat. His teeth-bared expression was wild and disoriented.

With an exclamation, Lauren ripped her seat belt apart and thrust herself into the executive's path. Mom's high-pitched squeal followed her. The elderly executive swatted at her as she reached for him. Panic must be driving him. The guy was clearly not rational. She just needed to shove him into his place and—

The plane delivered a fresh heave. With a howl, the executive staggered and toppled backward. A distinct *thunk* announced his head connecting with the edge of an extended guest table on the way down. Lauren lost her footing and tumbled down atop him. His doughy middle softened her fall, but her nose was buried in his bony chest. Senses heightened, conflicting odors assailed her—a hint of lavender laundry detergent and an exotic bergamot and tropical fruit cologne. An expensive brand, if she was not mistaken.

That rapid speed bump sensation continued

as Lauren struggled to her knees. "Help me get him into his seat," she cried to the other executives.

They stared at her, shaking their heads. A pair of dainty hands intruded into her line of vision. Mom. Together they fought for balance and wrestled the older man's limp body into his chair, fastened his belt and put the gas mask around his face. He was alive, Lauren knew that much, but she had no time to assess him medically.

She grabbed her mother's slender arm and propelled her toward their places. Mom plopped into hers and began buckling herself in, her entire body shivering. Lauren lifted her foot to return to her seat, but the plane took a plunge downward, and she landed hard on her behind in the aisle. Her belly leaped into her throat.

The plane continued to dive, and Lauren slid down the plush carpeting toward the cockpit. Then her hind end hit something that halted her. Bracing herself with a grip on the cabinetry of the galley, she swiveled her head. A pair of feet sticking out into the aisle had halted her slide. Her gaze followed the legs attached to the feet until she found the bloodied face of the copilot where she slumped, unconscious—or worse—up against the exit door behind the galley.

The plane bucked and shuddered, leveling off at a more or less horizontal angle. Lauren rose to her hands and knees. Her face was practically in the cockpit, where she noted the pilot remained firmly in his chair. At least someone was still trying to control this plane, but the utter blackness of the instrument panel was less than reassuring.

"I can hold 'er steady for maybe thirty seconds," Kent Garland's deep voice boomed, muffled slightly by an air mask. "Can you get Mags buckled into a seat in the passenger area?"

"Ma-a-ags?" The word quavered between Lauren's lips. *Oh, the copilot.* "I— I'll try."

"Good girl."

Girl! I'll girl him.

Anger sent fuel to her limbs. Lauren grabbed the copilot's shoulders and wrestled her into a vacant seat. She had no idea if the woman was alive, but on the off chance they survived the next minutes, she tightened the buckle around the copilot's waist and fitted the mask around her bloodied face. With shaking hands, Lauren pulled the bright-colored scarf from around the woman's neck and bound it tightly around her head, covering the gash near the woman's temple. That was the best she could do at this moment.

"Holler at everyone to get their heads down between their knees." Garland's bellow barely carried above the intensifying whine of struggling engines and the screams of terrified passengers. "Then take Mags's place beside me in the cockpit. Hurry!"

Gripping the seatback in front of her, Lauren yelled the pilot's instructions then turned and flung herself into the copilot's spot. She fastened the seat belt and jerked the mask tight around her face. Oxygen filled her lungs and cleared all clutter from her mind.

Silence suddenly flooded the cockpit as engine noise ceased. Even the passenger cabin had gone eerily quiet, as if every person aboard were holding their breaths. The side of a mountain filled the front window, racing toward them at breakneck speed.

"Lord Jesus," Lauren whispered, "ready or not, here I come."

Kent's muscles ached and his head pounded as he fought to keep the plane's nose up against the battering of powerful air currents. If they went into a nosedive, they'd implode onto the side of that mountain. In order to maintain any semblance of control, he had to hold the plane's glide even as he lost altitude. The best he could do was keep her level while the thermals bucked them around like a bee-stung bronco.

The fuel was gone. Whatever took out the avionics and wounded the engines had also damaged the fuel lines. His Challenger 350 had bled out in mere minutes. He could just barely buy that something might go wrong with one of the engines—some tiny little something overlooked. But both of them at once? *Uh-uh!* Not a snowball's chance in Hawaii. He took better care of this baby than that.

Kent's gaze darted toward his instruments, but the panel remained dark and dead, even though the RAT—ram air turbine—must have kicked in as an alternate source of electricity. Something was seriously bent about this flight emergency. There was nothing within normal range about it.

At least it was daylight so he had visual on where they were headed. If he could spot a valley with a decent stretch of level ground and navigate toward it, they stood a slight chance of actually landing without becoming a pile of wreckage—a nonsurvivable pile, anyway.

Somehow, he had to radio in a mayday. Get

their position out to someone who could send rescue. But there was no way he could release the stick with even one hand in order to use the radio. Unless... He glanced sideways.

The passenger in the copilot seat gripped her chair arms in clawed fists. Her torso quivered, and her gaze was fixed straight ahead, but at least she wasn't hysterical. Not hardly. She'd kept her cool and managed to get Mags buckled into a seat under terrifying conditions.

"Any chance you know how to operate a two-way radio?" His voice came out strong but muffled by the oxygen mask.

Seconds ticked past. Was she frozen in shock? Then she slowly turned her head his way. Brilliant green eyes, clear and sharp as a cat's, fixed on him.

"Y-yes. W-we use one in the hospital for medivac emergencies."

"Put out a distress call. Frequency, one-two-one-point-five."

She did as he had asked. Her hands, her whole being, seemed to center and go steady as she set the frequency and put out the call. Evidently, she was the kind that calmed when given a task in an emergency. Good characteristic. She performed the mayday drill once...

twice…three times. Dead air met every attempt. Those green eyes sought him again.

"I—I don't think the radio…" A spasm visibly gripped her throat. "The radio is dead." The sentence came out in a high squeak.

Kent's jaw clenched. "This has to be sabotage, pure and simple," he muttered fiercely between his teeth.

But who? Why? Terrorism? Unlikely on a small plane in the middle of nowhere. Terrorists wanted to make a big statement, spread as much fear and death as possible with a highly public act of chaos. What then? Did someone want to kill one of his passengers badly enough to take the life of everyone aboard?

Fury surged through Kent, shooting adrenaline to the taxed muscles laboring to control an out-of-control airplane. He and his passengers were going to survive, if only to give him the chance to throttle whoever was trying to kill them.

Responding to his iron grip, the plane steadied even as a promising furrow in the mountainside appeared off to his left. He followed his instinct and turned her nose for what could be a navigable valley.

"Hallelujah!" His outburst drew a startled stare from Jade Eyes.

A long, semi-flat stretch of ground appeared in the near distance. Scattered pine trees set up potential hazards, but he'd just have to do his best to miss them. They were coming in too fast, but this was the most optimal valley for landing that he'd spotted since the crisis erupted. It was either bring her down now or crash in harsh terrain with no chance of survival.

There would be nothing graceful about this landing. With no engine power, he had no reverse thrust or flaps to help slow them down. Getting on the ground without flipping over or hitting anything major would have to be enough. Now it remained to be seen if they'd have to come in on their bare belly. If electrical failure were absolute, they'd have no wheels.

Kent barked orders to his unofficial copilot, instructing her how to let down the landing gear. A welcome rumble under the plane's belly answered her tentative responses to his instructions. The instrument panel was not receiving any of the auxiliary electricity, but the landing gear was. Another anomaly that suggested sabotage focused on his engines and his instrumentation.

Kent hauled in a deep breath and let it out as the ground loomed up at them. "Get your head down, Jade Eyes!"

"What did you call me?" Those brilliant eyes flashed, and her nostrils flared.

"Get! Down!"

The woman bowed her back and hugged her knees as the wheels kissed the earth. The plane rebounded into the air like a gazelle, then slammed down again. Up. Down. Up. Down. The odor of burning rubber invaded the cockpit. Stretched and strained metal screeched like a dying thing, competing with the terrified screams from human throats.

All the peripherals faded as Kent's consciousness melded with his tortured plane. Any chance of survival depended on his skills and instincts as a former Special Forces pilot and the grace of Almighty God.

If the former failed, in about 30 seconds they'd all be meeting the Lord face-to-face.

TWO

A long groan hauled Lauren to consciousness. Who made that sound? A moan passed between her lips. Oh, *she'd* made that sound. No, the first groan had been in a male timbre.

Lauren lifted her head, and pain sparkled through her muscles. A spot on the top of her head throbbed. What had happened? Bits of something skittered out of her hair. Glass? Twigs? Needles? Maybe all three. A shredded pine branch drooped forlornly in front of her face, nearly tickling her chin.

She drew in a deep, pine-laden breath and examined herself. Glass littered her short-sleeved, pullover top and jeans, and glinted in the sunlight beating through the shattered windshield. Scratches on the bare forearms that had protected her head oozed small beads of blood, but the injuries weren't serious.

Lauren shivered. The sun had power, and yet she was chilled. If she had to guess, the temperature was somewhere in the fifties Fahrenheit. A stiff breeze whimpered through the cockpit.

Cockpit!

She stiffened, muscles grumbling at the sudden movement. She'd been in an airplane crash. Where were they? Clearly, on the ground somewhere in the mountains. Dusty greenish landscape stretched in front of her, punctuated by some brown, man-made looking structures in the distance. The whole vista was framed by dark cliff walls.

Had they crashed near a town? Was help on the way? Watery haze coated her vision, but she blinked it away. Nothing approaching human life or technology, like a car or ambulance or fire engine, raced toward them from the structures. Except for the tick of cooling machinery somewhere in the plane's bowels and the lonely keen of the wind, silence reigned.

Was she the only survivor? *Mom!* A shudder ran through Lauren as her hands fumbled for the clip of the seat belt. The masculine groan came again. Gingerly, she turned her head to find Kent Garland slumped in his seat. Blood trickled from somewhere beneath the sable-brown hair just above his ear, but his eyes were open.

Amazement flooded her. Somehow this man had landed the plane. She had no recollection of the event, but that was not surprising in cases where someone was knocked unconscious.

"Help!" a male voice called weakly from the passenger area. Other voices began making unintelligible noises that communicated fear and pain. They all sounded masculine. Was her mother all right?

Garland grunted and lifted his head. His gaze clashed with Lauren's. She sucked in a breath. A woman could float away in those cloud-gray depths.

"We're down." His lips stretched in a grimace. "Time for evac and damage assessment. You up to helping, Jade Eyes?"

His words were spoken with a teasing lilt, but a sharp pang streaked through Lauren, trampled quickly by anger. She swallowed the knee-jerk response. This man couldn't know what he had said.

"Don't call me that, Mr. Garland. My name is Lauren Carter." She couldn't help it if her tone was frosty.

"Okay, Lauren." A smile twitched one side of the pilot's mouth, but his gaze remained grave. "Call me Kent. Are you all right?"

"I—I think so." She cleared her throat. "I'm

a physician's assistant. If you have a first-aid kit, I'll do what I can to treat the injured."

The pilot's eyes widened. "That's the first good news I've heard since...well, a while." The barest hint of private pain flickered across his face, and then his expression went flat. "Let's get to it."

He threw off his seat belt and wriggled free of the forward control panel that had crumpled inward significantly, but not enough to trap him. "I seem to be in working order." He stood tall and lifted one slacks-clad leg and then the other.

Lauren levered herself to her feet. Other than adrenaline-withdrawal tremors flowing through her body and perhaps bruises she would feel more intensely later on, she seemed to be in working order as well. Except maybe for that bump on her head. She touched her fingertips to a throbbing goose egg on the crown of her head. The skin didn't appear to be broken. Judging from the momentary loss of consciousness, she probably had some level of concussion. Hopefully mild. She needed to be able to function.

"Mom!" she called out. No answer and no tawny-gray head popped up anywhere above the seats.

Lauren pressed forward, but the pilot stepped

in front of her just as a bulky executive lunged to his feet and lumbered toward them, head down like a charging rhino.

"We've got to get out of here." Hysteria edged the man's tone. "We're going to blow up!"

More passengers began struggling to their feet, echoing the terrified thought.

"Hold it!" Kent's authoritative voice sliced through the panic. "We are down safe, and we are *not* going to blow up. Stay in your seats. When it comes to evacuation, we'll do it together. Let's get our bearings first."

The panicked rhino plunged to a stop, chest heaving.

"How do you know we're not going to explode?" cried another passenger, voice high and tight.

"Simple. It takes fuel to fire an explosion. We don't have any."

Lauren bit her lower lip. That explained the necessity of a crash landing, but not what blew up and caused the fuel dump and the instrument/radio failure. That was something she wanted an answer for ASAP, but not while people were teetering on the verge of hysteria.

At the rear of the plane, a blistering tirade of profanity burst from one of the three Peerless One brokers. He was standing tall, holding his cell phone toward the ceiling, shaking it and cursing it.

"What seems to be the problem, sir?" Kent asked briskly.

"No cell service, that's what." The pit-bull-faced man scowled like a juicy steak had just been ripped from his jaws. "I was meeting with an important client tonight, and now I can't let him know our incompetent pilot has crashed this tin can you call a plane. I'll lose the account!"

"Get a grip, Dirk," said one of the other Peerless One executives. "It's amazing that we're alive."

Still scowling, the man named Dirk plopped back into his seat and silence fell, except for a few sniffles and groans.

Lauren gazed around Kent's shoulders, searching for her mother. Anxious faces stared back at her above freshly rumpled three-piece suits. The elder statesman of the group was stirring and coming around to consciousness. But the spot where her mother had sat appeared to be empty. Of course, a seatback largely blocked her view.

Lauren's heart sought to pump out of her chest. "Where's my mother?"

Kent began moving up the aisle, nudging personal items under seats with his foot. "I'll look for her. Not much room to go very far. Would you please check on my copilot?"

Lauren's breath snagged. She'd forgotten about the critically injured woman. What kind of a physician's assistant was she? Apparently, the kind that was a daughter first.

She stepped into the first set of seats, bent over the slumped woman and felt for a pulse. It was there, ragged and faint, but at least Mags was alive. Gently, Lauren lowered the seat back as far as it would go and padded each side of the woman's head with one of those little airliner pillows. That should give the injured woman some support for her back and neck. Moving her could be tricky if she had a spinal injury.

"What is Mags's status?" Kent's voice called back to her.

"I would say concussion—probably severe—but the bleeding on the external head wound appears to have stopped. I'll take a closer look in the near future and suture the cut, if necessary, but that's about the extent of what I can do without expert diagnostic equipment. If she has a subdural hematoma— a brain bleed—she will need surgery, and I can't…I'm not…"

Lauren inhaled sharply against a surge of frustration. A subdural hematoma was life-threatening. There certainly was no X-ray machine or other diagnostic equipment around here, much less any surgical tools with which to perform a craniotomy, even if she were qualified to perform one, which a PA-C was not. They needed expert help. Fast!

"Just do your best," Kent responded. "That's all any of us can do. Your mom's right here!"

Kent's call brought Lauren's head up. Her mother's pixie face peeped around her seat, pale but composed.

Mom flapped a hand. "Sorry, dear. I guess I passed out."

Lauren grabbed for the support of a seat-back. Now she could testify it was no cliché that knees did go weak when major relief hit. "It's okay, Mom. Are you hurt anywhere?"

"Just my pride… I think. Well, no. I'm pretty sure that seat belt gave the old college try at cutting me in half. My tummy hurts, but I'm sure it will pass."

Lauren didn't like the sound of that. Mom could have anything from a ruptured spleen to kidney damage. Or maybe just some bruising and tissue abrasions, but that was best-case scenario. And again, there didn't seem to be any emergency facilities nearby. Perhaps no life at all. She gazed over her shoulder through the shattered windshield and scanned the barren landscape beyond. If that was a town out there, it appeared to be deserted. Hopefully, appearances were deceiving.

She turned toward Kent, who eyed her from the rear of the plane. "Are we going to get people as comfortable as possible here, or could some help be available in that nearby town?"

Garland exhaled a brief chuckle. "I'm fairly certain no one is home in whatever is left of that old mining burg, but I'm going to go check it out. If there's decent shelter or any kind of supplies, we might move in there until help arrives."

Voices streamed questions about who might be coming to rescue them and when and how, but the pilot lifted a silencing hand. "All unknowns at this point. I'll go check out the town while you allow our resident PA to check out your injuries." He nodded toward Lauren. "The first-aid kit is in the galley."

"What about your head wound?" Lauren asked. "I should look at that before you go hiking."

Striding up the aisle toward her, Kent shrugged a shoulder. "Just a nick from flying glass. Look after these fine folks first." He brushed past her, opened a bin, and pulled out a leather bomber jacket that looked like it had seen better days.

Lauren pressed her lips together. Stubborn macho man. So not her type. Then why did her pulse speed up as he shrugged the coat over broad shoulders?

Frowning, he turned his attention to the main exit behind the cockpit. The door panel looked like an accordion. Fat chance it would open. Lauren's insides curdled. The way the body of the plane was twisted and bent, how stable was it? Could something give way at any time?

Kent sent her a sidelong look, as if he'd heard her thoughts, and headed back down the aisle. "I'm going to use the emergency exit over the wing."

With practiced movements, he pulled out the panel and leaned it up against a sidewall.

"One of you fit this back in after I hop out."

Kent glanced around the cabin, gaze lighting briefly on Lauren. His face was an impassive mask, but in his eyes lurked a grim shadow. Then he hauled himself through the opening.

A chill wind blew through the cabin, and a couple of the executives hopped up and hastily stuffed the door panel back into the opening. The pilot's disappearance triggered a burst of complaints from the passengers about the cold and demands that Lauren take a look at them immediately. Everyone claimed to have one pitiful condition or another.

"I'll get to all of you," Lauren said firmly, "but first I'm going to do a little triage and see who is most critically injured, other than the copilot, who is as comfortable as I can make her at the moment."

The only executive not trying to whine himself to the head of the line was the elderly one who had finally come fully awake. He gazed around quietly, rubbing the back of his head, and looking thoroughly unhappy.

Her mother smiled and shrugged. "You can see me last, dear. I'm all right."

The others might be high-powered wheeler-dealers who lived each day on the rush of stock trades and business deals, but actual physical danger or discomfort rendered them dependent children. Sighing, Lauren hunted up the first-aid kit.

What was that pilot not telling them? He had said nothing about contacting the outside world. He sure hadn't indicated rescue was imminent. His instrument panel was dead. The radio, too. Surely, he'd filed a flight plan before they'd taken off. When the aircraft didn't arrive at its destination, search parties would look for them. Right? They would be found. Lauren's gut tightened. But what if they weren't?

Insides hollow, Kent stood on the ground and surveyed the remains of his business jet. This narrow valley was sure no landing strip. As soon as he'd hit ground, rocks and potholes and the odd pine sapling that he couldn't avoid had begun doing things to his plane that never should be done to fine machinery.

He'd slewed once so badly that his left wing gouged the earth, and they'd done a doughnut before finally straightening out. A good chunk of wing tip remained embedded in the ground somewhere along his landing path. And the landing gear was chewed up but good. The forward wheel was missing entirely, and the rear two were in shreds. The twisted body of the plane rested mostly on bare metal struts. Those were only the most obvious structural issues.

His jaw clenched against a sting in the back of his eyes. His jet was less than a year old. A real beaut! His pride and joy. Every nickel he had in the world was tied up in his baby, and now look at her!

Kent cleared his throat and inhaled a deep breath. At least he and his passengers had survived the crazy descent and landing. He should be thanking God, not wallowing in angst. Besides which, he had a mystery to solve. What happened to bring them down in the first place?

"I'd like to be the first to thank you for getting us on the ground safely."

Lauren's voice drew his attention, and he lifted his head. She stood framed in the broken window of the cockpit, hugging the first-aid kit to her chest. Kent's pulse rate skipped into overdrive. She looked vulnerable and tense, but calm and determined and...well, flat gorgeous. Wavy strands of auburn hair had come loose from her thick ponytail and framed a heart-shaped face. The strong chin and elegant, aquiline nose suggested the courage she'd already displayed, but the soft curves of her full mouth and delicately shaped eyebrows lent appealing femininity.

"Earth to Kent." Her small, teasing smile sent a pleasant shiver down his spine.

He blinked and threw off the fascination. What was the matter with him, anyway? Must be the stress of the emergency landing.

"You're most welcome," he said. "Life or death is a great motivator."

"That's for sure." Her gaze darkened. "I

see you're studying the plane. Any clues as to what brought us down?"

He shook his head. "Too soon to say."

"So, you're not certain it was sabotage?"

Kent narrowed his eyes. That was all he needed to ramp up the hysteria among the passengers—the suggestion that someone was out to get them. Even if someone might be. "Who mentioned anything like that?"

"You did."

"No, I—" Kent shut his jaw and hauled a crisp, pine-rich breath through his nose. Maybe he *had* mumbled his thoughts out loud in the heat of the moment. "Look, let's get everyone to whatever shelter we can find before we start assigning blame."

"I'm not interested in blame." Her tone had sharpened. "I'm interested in truth, and everyone on this aircraft has a right to know why we crash-landed in the Rockies instead of touching down smoothly in San Francisco."

"I'm as interested in those answers as you are, but first things first."

She offered him a cool nod. "But you'll tell us when you know, right?"

"I'll tell you what I find as soon as I find it as soon as I think it's wise for everyone to know."

"That's too convoluted for me." Her eyes shot green fire.

He waved and tromped toward the old mining town. Jade Eyes wasn't happy with his non-answer, but there was no use promising something he wasn't sure he could deliver. It was possible that he might not be able to nail down the cause by simply eyeballing the damage. Professional examination with diagnostic tools might be necessary. Then again, he might know in a heartbeat as soon as he got to the source of the damage. But even then, there might be facts he'd be prudent to keep under his hat until he could talk to the proper authorities.

Stuffing his hands into the pockets of his bomber jacket, Kent hunched his shoulders against the bite of the wind sideswiping him. The jacket did a nice job of keeping his torso warm, but his neck and ears stung with the cold.

How was he going to transport eight people, some of them injured, the quarter mile or so from the plane to the dubious shelter of these old mining structures? But as sure as they were all still in the land of the living that was what would have to be done. Sooner, rather than later. The perforated metal tube that remained of his aircraft would turn mighty cold, mighty fast, especially when night fell, and the temps were likely to be in the forties or even the thirties. They were below the perpetual snowline here, and by the green yet showing in certain vegetation, a hard frost had not yet hit, but winter was closing in like a wolf after a rabbit.

Kent shuddered. He didn't want to think about being stuck here in this barren patch of the Rockies long enough for winter to pounce. At least in town, they would have the option of lighting a fire—maybe they'd even find a pot-bellied stove to hunker around. The plane had skimmed over the top of a sparkling stream during their landing, and the water was likely potable; what they'd eat was another question. The rations aboard the plane weren't all that plentiful—leftover chicken salad croissants and Caesar salad from the onboard lunch Mags had served, water, soft drinks and assorted bags of snacks. Yup. They'd eat well... until tomorrow.

At least he could be thankful for a medical practitioner among the passengers. Lauren Carter was sure a surprise—in more ways than one. Gutsy to the point of foolhardy. A bit prickly about certain things, like her proper name and direct answers when she asked a question, but if Mags survived, she'd owe Lauren big-time.

Magdalena Haven, a flight crew member from his US Air Force days, had been Kent's copilot for the last six months. She was energetic and skilled. Not always the most upbeat person, but life couldn't be easy for her, coping with her medical bills from last year's car accident, not to mention her recent bitter divorce. And now his comrade-in-arms was injured again. He shook his head and said a prayer.

Trudging onward, Kent pushed away the image of Mags's bloodied face. Lauren's image sharpened in its place, and his gut twisted. Why did the woman have to be so attractive? Not just physically, but the courage and dependability she'd shown was...well, a lot more than he'd ever seen in Elspeth.

Elspeth with a p *and most definitely not Elizabeth.* His almost-mother-in-law's lofty tones slithered through his mind, and Kent shuddered with an entirely different kind of cold than atmospheric conditions could produce. No, thank you. If Lauren was under the thumb of a domineering mother, any attraction he felt for her would never be explored.

What had Mrs. Barrington murmured to him as she boarded? Oh, yeah.

Marlin speaks highly of you, young man. You may notice that I am traveling with a very attractive, single *daughter. We'll be staying at the Ritz-Carlton.*

Kent snorted. What a whopper! Marlin Barrington had his own personal jet that he flew around in. Only occasionally did the man's firm charter additional transportation, and the senior executive was certainly not involved in the transaction. That sort of thing was done by an administrative assistant. Besides, Mags had taken the reservation. A Wall Street tycoon like Marlin Barrington wouldn't know him from Adam, so how could he have an opinion about Kent's character? If Mrs. Barrington was fishing that desperately for a catch for her daughter, there was no way he was going to rise to the bait. No matter how appealing that bait might be.

He slowed his stride as he reached the scattering of wooden structures. The first building was set a short way out from the others and had the look of a livery stable in the barn-like structure and the broken-down remains of a corral attached to one side. Maybe, just maybe, some type of wheeled vehicle might be found inside. Even a wheelbarrow would be better than nothing.

"Don't hold your breath," he muttered to

himself as he pulled on the handle of one side of the stable's double doors.

The handle came off in his hand. *No!* The entire door was coming down. With a yelp, Kent dodged the falling slab of wood. The door whumped to the ground, sending a puff of dirt into the windy air.

He coughed and shook his head. "Well, that's one way to get a look inside."

Kent stepped over the threshold into twilight. The air smelled musty, and dust motes danced in shafts of light squeezing through cleaner patches in dirt-coated window panes. It was significantly warmer in here than outside.

He moved further into the building. Rotting leather tack dangled from hooks here and there. Empty box stalls lined two sides of a wide aisle. Any hay or straw that was left behind had long since turned into piles of dust that swirled around on the residue of wind that invaded the place through the open door. A sneeze racked his body. If any of his passengers had allergies, this would *not* be the place for them to stay. He'd better check out some of the other buildings before he went back to the plane.

What was the bulky object in the far corner?

Kent hurried past the stalls. Here, a larger area must have housed buggies or wagons.

Only one remained—an enclosed boxy contraption, narrow, with a high seat for the driver out front, but no doors in the sides. He walked around the wagon, pulling on each iron-shod wheel as he went. They seemed solid enough. Two lines of faded lettering graced each long side, but it was too dim inside the stable to read what they said. The entrance door to the interior of the carriage was in the back. Some kind of prison wagon? If so, where were the bars?

Shaking his head, he hefted the wooden beam to which a team of horses or oxen would have been attached and pulled. The axles let out a high screech but the wheels began to turn.

Kent's heart lightened. He wouldn't be able to transport everyone in the same load. Not enough room. Besides, he was strong, but he was no horse. Still, it shouldn't take more than a few trips to get the people, as well as blankets, pillows, food, beverages and other useful items into town. Hopefully, his battered passengers would take comfort in small mercies.

Kent managed with little trouble to get the strange carriage out into the sunlight. He stood back to take a better look at his prize. Now he could easily read the words painted on the sides, faded as they were. His pulse stalled as their meaning slapped him in the jaw.

Property of Undertaker.
Trouble Creek, Nevada.
This wagon was going to be no comfort to anyone. No comfort at all.

THREE

"Young lady, my head is harder than most bowling balls." The older executive glared up at Lauren from his cushy seat, age-spotted hands folded over his modest paunch. "I don't need to be poked and prodded."

"Sir, a concussion is all about the softness of your brain slamming around *inside* that bowling ball." She frowned down at him. "I do need to perform some basic assessment."

The edges of the curmudgeon's lips curved upward. "Deftly done, young lady. I am put in my place." The smile grew, revealing even rows of gleaming, white teeth. Dentures, no doubt, since his speech carried the slight slur that sometimes came with that territory. "Very well, you may shine your little flashlight into my pupils and confirm that they are equal in size and reactive."

Lauren lifted her eyebrows. "You have medical training?"

"No, I just watched a lot of *Dr. Kildare* in my younger years."

"Who?"

"Never mind, well before your time." He removed thick-lensed glasses and stared up at her with shrewd, brown eyes.

Lauren scanned his pupils with the penlight she had found in the medical kit. "At least as far as this symptom of concussion, you have a clean bill of health, Mr... Ah."

"Gleason. But you may call me Neil."

"Are you related to Jackie?"

Neil Gleason let out a raspy chuckle. "Not at all. You may not be familiar with my favorite TV doc, but I see you're not out of the loop on all prehistoric television personalities."

Lauren smiled. "My grandmother loved *The Honeymooners.* I watched a few reruns with her when I was little. And you may call me Lauren, rather than young lady."

"It's a deal. Now feel free to assess someone needier that I. Your mother, perhaps?"

"Thank you. I'll do that."

She began packing up her kit. It was actually amazing that she wasn't dealing with a whole gamut of major medical problems, instead of an abundance of minor ones. She'd examined every passenger except her mom, and doctored cuts and contusions from flying objects. While one of her patients had a broken finger from trying to protect his head from said objects, thankfully no one was bleeding profusely from a slice through a vein or an artery. As for more serious injuries, she suspected kneecap fracture or dislocation in Richard, the next oldest to Neil, but the best she could do in the confines of the jet was wrap the limb and apply an ice pack.

Lauren found her mother hugging herself, frowning and staring out the window.

"Are you in pain?" Lauren bent over her.

"Not really." She dredged up a faint smile. "I'm starting to feel cold, though. With the cockpit windshield gone and my jacket packed away in the stowed luggage, there's not much between us and the great outdoors. Looks pretty barren out there. No snow yet in this valley, but it's coming soon. I can feel it."

"I'll grab one of those airplane blankets for you after I palpate your abdomen."

"You're going to do what?"

Lauren chuckled. "I'm going to press on your tummy in different spots to see if you hurt somewhere specific."

"Whew! At least you're not contemplating surgery." Mom winked up at her.

Lauren's heart squeezed in upon itself. What if her mother did have an internal injury that required surgery? What if some of her other patients had something like that going on, and the issue hadn't yet been identified? For sure, Mags needed to be hospitalized immediately. There was so little Lauren could do out in the middle of nowhere with nothing but a first-aid kit.

Mom squeezed her arm. "I'm fine, dear."

The warm touch pumped encouragement into Lauren's bloodstream. "Go ahead and put your seat all the way back while I check you out."

Her mother complied, and Lauren swiftly determined that the ache was general across the length of abdomen where the seat belt had fastened, and no point of pressure elicited a sharp pain. Good signs that the damage was muscle strain and bruising, not damage to an internal organ. Still, she'd keep her mother under close observation.

"I think you may live," Lauren concluded with a wink, and her mother laughed. "Now, about that blanket," she swiveled on her heels, "I'll— Oops!" She halted barely in time to keep from bumping into one of the executives.

The man's angular face sported a butterfly bandage closing a long, shallow cut on his cheek and a purple goose egg on his jaw, which Lauren believed was not broken, only bruised. The tall, raw-boned man held a small stack of blankets.

"Take one of these," he said. "I was just going to start passing them out. None of us brought our outdoor jackets on board. They're all packed away with the luggage."

"Mr. Yancy, isn't it?" Lauren accepted the blanket. "Thank you for thinking of this."

He offered a small smile. "Call me Cliff. Now that the edge is off the hysteria, I think we can start functioning like intelligent human beings who are grateful to be alive."

"Here he comes!" Mom called out, angling her head toward the outside.

"Who's coming?" a passenger demanded sharply from farther back in the plane. "Are we being rescued?"

"It's our hero pilot, who has already rescued us from sudden death, so let's see what new and amazing trick he's pulled out of his hat." Mom pointed out the window.

"All I want to know is when a chopper will be arriving to get us back to civilization," a surly voice grumbled.

Lauren identified it as coming from Dirk Dixon, the man with the broken finger and the foul mouth. She felt the same way about being rescued as soon as possible, but a male diva attitude wasn't going to help make it happen.

She leaned across a vacant seat toward a window and gaped at her mother's freshly anointed hero and whatever strange vehicle he was dragging behind him. Not that everyone aboard didn't owe Kent Garland a world of gratitude and no little admiration for his skill as a pilot, but if Mom thought she could put stars in Lauren's eyes about this guy or any other, she was doomed to disappointment.

The pilot brought the contraption to a stop next to the wing, and Lauren got a look at the words painted on the side. What? He'd found a hearse? She shivered. The cold must be getting to her, because she was in no way superstitious about a dusty old wagon.

She turned and smacked her palms together. "All right, people. I believe our chariot has arrived."

"I'm getting out of here." The man with the broken finger jumped to his feet.

"Mr. Dixon, we will evacuate the most seriously injured first."

The man smirked and held up his bandaged hand.

A pop announced the emergency exit panel turning loose, and Kent stuck his head through the opening.

"That means my copilot, Magdalena Haven," he said firmly, "as well as Ms. Carter to watch over her, and then the rest of you will go in whatever order her triage assessment dictates."

His icy stare toward Dixon brooked no argument. The executive scowled and sat down.

"Next after Mags and me should be Richard Engle," Lauren said. "His leg needs more attention than I can give it in here. Both of those patients will need to lie flat, so I think that's all for the first load. Phil Blount and Dirk Dixon will be for the next load in order of triage. Then I want Neil Gleason, Cliff Yancy and my mother." She nodded toward Kent.

"I'll help do the mule thing." A tentative hand went up from Cliff.

"And I can walk. So they won't have to pull me," said Phil, the bulky man who'd given way to panic in the first moments after landing. "That way, Neil and Mrs. Barrington can go in the second load, too."

The man had been sheepish ever since his display of terror. Lauren sent him a smile, and he drew himself up tall, dignity restored.

"Sounds like a plan," said Kent. "First, round up as many of the blankets and pillows as you can. Keep whatever you need for yourselves for the trip, but send the rest in the first load. We're also going to harvest the seat cushions. Grab some of those now for the most injured to lie on."

Healthy activity began in the cabin of what was once a luxury aircraft. With something constructive to do, the tension in the passengers seemed to ease. If only Lauren could say the same for herself. She'd never looked after patients under such primitive conditions. The prognosis for the copilot was not good if help didn't reach them soon. And who knew what complications might develop in her other patients?

Shoving her jitters to the back of her mind, Lauren threw herself into aiding people and organizing supplies. Moving Mags was the most delicate operation. They formed a makeshift sling out of blankets and somehow managed to get her limp form out the egress window. Cliff and Phil had already gone outside to help Kent, and the three of them easily slid her onto a set of cushions in the back of the black ambulance. Lauren refused to think of it as a hearse.

Transferring Richard Engle was almost more difficult, because the man flinched and moaned with every jostle. Not that she blamed him. He had an excruciating injury and had behaved better about it than certain others with minor hurts. Finally, her turn came, and she climbed out the window onto the wing of the plane. She began shivering immediately, despite the blanket around her shoulders.

Standing between the wing and the open door of the ambulance, Kent reached up and took her hand, steadying her as she leaped to the ground. His grip sent a tingle up her arm, and his encouraging smile warmed her straight down to her toes. *All right. Enough of that nonsense.* She made herself look away and climbed into the wagon with her patients—one inert and comatose, the other gritting his teeth and stifling groans.

If only she had something stronger for pain than the limited stock of non-narcotic analgesics in the first-aid kit. The kit contained things like nitroglycerin and epinephrine designed to respond to medical emergencies in-flight, not deal with injuries due to a crash landing.

The inside of the wagon smelled stale and musty. Lauren wrinkled her nose as she settled cross-legged between her patients. Someone closed the door, and darkness swooped in. Only a few small cracks in the wood allowed slivers of dull sunlight to ease the gloom.

"How are you doing, Mr. Engle?" she asked.

"Call me Rich, please, and I'm alive. Guess that will have to be enough for now."

"Hang in there. The emergency kit contains

lidocaine for local anesthetic. Once we get to an environment where I have room to work, I'll administer it. If your kneecap is only dislocated, I should be able to put it back in place, which will decrease your pain level, longterm. There is some risk of aggravating possible cartilage damage, but—"

Her patient wheezed a small laugh. "Anything to ease the pain sounds great to me."

Their wagon creaked and shifted.

"Here we go." She patted Rich's arm.

Rocking and jouncing in a vehicle with no shock absorbers went on for a small eternity. Finally, they stopped and the door swung wide. Kent stood framed in the opening. He was puffing, and a trickle of sweat traced a path from his left brow to his chin, but the white cloud of his breath testified to the chill in the air. When the sun went down, chilly would become downright cold. They had a lot to accomplish in the few hours before sunset.

Lauren pulled her blanket tighter around her and stepped down out of the wagon. They were parked in front of a weathered clapboard structure with a sagging porch and very few intact windows. The faded sign over the building announced it as the Trouble Creek Mercantile. Whatever supplies the mercantile had stocked were bound to be long gone. Trouble Creek had been abandoned for quite a while.

"Doesn't look like much," Kent said with a wave toward the shabby building, "but I've laid down sturdy boards from the steps to the door so none of us is going to fall through on our way inside. The structure is sound, though I can't guarantee the roof doesn't leak. But if we can scrounge things up to cover the broken window panes, the potbellied stove in the middle of the front room should warm us up considerably. No lack of old wood for fuel around here."

"You've thought of a lot of things in a little time." Lauren beamed up at her mom's pilot hero.

The guy certainly had a good head on those impressive shoulders. It might be interesting to get to know him better—not as a boyfriend, of course, but as a person. He probably had a thing for his copilot anyway, judging by how protective he acted toward her.

Kent's gaze dropped toward his feet. "Just doing what I can."

Lauren narrowed her eyes. "What is it that you don't want to tell us you *can't* do?"

His lips pulled tight beneath grim eyes. "Let's get everyone transferred safely, and then we'll all have a powwow."

Simmering, Lauren barely restrained herself from stomping across the porch boards. Aggravating man. One thing Lauren had learned to hate in her early years—other people deciding when to tell her things she was entitled to know. All she wanted was straight answers to important questions…even though everything she dreaded might be in those answers.

Kent tromped toward the downed plane, empty wagon in tow. He'd left Phil and Cliff with Lauren and her patients to see if they could get that stove going, as well as find ways to cover the broken window panes.

On this next trip back to town, Dirk could walk or even help him pull. That measly broken finger didn't qualify him for a free ride. Phil had told him they called the guy DJ at Peerless One where they worked together. The nickname drove Dirk nuts, because he thought they were referring to his brief and unstellar career as a disc jockey in the nightclubs before he made it in arbitrage. No one had ever told him the initials stood for Dirk the Jerk. Not hard to guess how he earned that name. Kent suppressed a grimace.

A half hour later, he helped Mrs. Barrington into the wagon. At her insistence, she was the last to climb aboard.

The dainty woman awarded him a large smile. "Thank you, sir," she said, "And please call me Nina. I can see you are among the last of the true gallants. I believe you have impressed even my headstrong daughter with your courtesy and service."

Kent shut the wagon door and shook his head. Impressed Lauren Carter? Aggravated would be more accurate. He seemed to have a gift for pushing her buttons.

He headed back toward town with the wagonload of people and supplies. Dirk Dixon plodded alongside him, wearing a scowl. Fat chance the guy would help him pull.

They arrived back at the abandoned general store to the tune of lively hammering. Was it possible the former inhabitants had left tools behind? Might there be other survival treasures lying around, too?

Kent smiled as he helped his passengers out of the wagon. Everyone—even Dirk—carried a load of food and other supplies inside the store. Kent placed himself last in line and stopped short just over the threshold.

Someone had brought order out of hodgepodge. He could about guess who. The fixed counter that sat on one side of the open area, as well as the moveable shelving, appeared to have been wiped off, though the floor remained thick with dust due to lack of a broom. The shelving had been arranged to afford both organized storage and a margin of privacy between the bulk of the room and the most critically injured passengers. He caught a glimpse of Lauren kneeling beside Mags, taking her pulse.

A fire blazed in the stove, and the building was already much warmer than when he'd left about an hour ago. Cushions were arranged on the floor around the stove to allow a little seating comfort up off the dirt on the floor.

Kent deposited his load of food and beverages on the glass-fronted shelving unit that was fixed to the floor and had probably served as the checkout counter. He gazed around at broken windows being covered with what looked like thin slabs of wood. Cliff turned from one of the windows and held up a shiny nail and a partially rusted crowbar, now serving as a hammer.

He grinned. "Found a sealed box of these." He wagged the nail. "And some old, empty crates in the back storage room. Busted up the crates. Found this on the floor," he lifted the crowbar, "and, voilà, wooden curtains."

"And I found these," Phil said, pointing to a pair of oil lamps on the counter. "No kerosene, though." He frowned.

"Maybe we'll run across some," Nina said and patted his arm. "Or some candles. In the meantime, I believe we are all due a break. How about some of these peanuts and pretzels and a soft drink for everyone?"

No one turned her down, especially not Kent. But water was his preferred beverage after all the exertion, and he wasn't done yet. One more trip today.

"We need to go get the luggage," he said. "The stove and wooden curtains are great, but we're still going to need our jackets and probably dress in layers to stay warm."

Lauren came around the wall of shelving and grabbed a bottle of water. Her clothes were dusty, and dirt smudged one cheek. Weariness etched small lines around her big, green eyes. How come the disarray, brought about by trauma and compassion, emphasized her attractiveness far more than Elspeth's haute couture ever had?

Lauren's gaze caught his, and his heart did a stupid skippy thing. A motion with her water bottle beckoned him to follow her. She led him into her makeshift hospital. Richard Engle had his eyes closed and appeared to be lying comfortably, though his leg was raised, resting on an extra cushion, and his knee was immobilized in bulky wrappings. The blood had been washed from Mags's face, and a towel-wrapped cold pack pressed against a spot on her head, but her complexion was waxen. She lay unnaturally still. Kent swallowed a lump in his throat.

"I managed to put Rich's kneecap back in place," Lauren said, "but Mags needs a doctor and a modern hospital immediately. I believe she's hemorrhaging inside her skull, which puts life-threatening pressure on her brain. Don't you think it's about time we know what chance there is of rescue happening anytime soon?"

Kent nodded. "Step out here. I'll talk to all of you at the same time."

They went back to the counter where the others were still snacking, and Kent cleared his throat. Attention was instantaneous and electric.

"I wish I could tell you that we will be rescued any minute now."

Dirk barked a laugh. "All these housekeeping preparations pretty much told us we're not looking for anyone today. So when *is* the cavalry coming? Tomorrow? Any later than that, and I can tell you it's going to cost Peerless One, and me personally, a bundle. That's unacceptable. We need to be—"

"Shut up!" Neil growled. "Lives are more

important than the next stock trade. How many companies do we represent here? At least three. But I guarantee you, in the big picture, our no-show within the next few days will wind up a minor hiccup in the big scheme of business. I'm on the fast track toward retirement, but I've been digging in my heels about taking the plunge. This little adventure has convinced me that it's time to let go of work, work, work, and enjoy life. When we return to civilization, my company will have to bid me *sayonara* for good."

"Everyone, hush, please." Lauren's voice quivered like a plucked violin string. "Right now, our pilot is the only one who has anything to say that we need to hear."

Kent's heart hovered somewhere around his toes. If only he could tell them what they wanted to hear. But truth was the only commodity worth trading in at this moment.

"I've flown under a lot of adverse conditions, but I've never heard of or experienced anything like what happened up there. My instruments, including the radio, went out in the blink of an eye. Something catastrophic happened to the plane."

"The explosion." Cliff jabbed the air with a nail. "Accidental malfunction or—"

"A bomb!" The hysterical edge had returned to Phil's voice. "Terrorists tried to kill us!"

"Whoa!" Kent held up a quieting hand. "Let's not get ahead of ourselves. Tomorrow I'll go over every inch of the plane, and then I might know more." His gaze skimmed the expectant faces. "But here's the thing. I can fly and land a plane without instruments. Had to do it under extremely tough conditions and on challenging terrain when I was in the air force, but I cannot promise to resurrect that radio. And even if I did, I have my doubts it would be able to communicate with the outside world."

"Why not?" Dirk demanded.

Kent pulled a small compass out of his pocket. He held it up so they could see the needle jumping all over the place. "The rocks coating the ground are taconite. I'm pretty sure this area was mined for iron. If there's enough metal around to confuse my compass, there's probably plenty left to scramble a radio signal. Maybe even to keep any signal from leaving this valley."

Phil wrung pudgy hands. "What about that black box thingy we hear about on the news? Doesn't that send a signal to a satellite when a plane crashes?"

"Same problem."

"In plain speech," Lauren said, tone flat, "no one knows where we are, and no one is coming to rescue us."

The proverbial pin-drop would easily have broken the silence. A nail plummeted from Cliff's hand and hit the floor with a noise like a sonic boom.

"Why can't a few of us just hike out of here and send help for the rest of you?" Neil's matter-of-fact tone breathed sanity back into the atmosphere. "This was a town. There must be a road in and out."

Kent frowned. "Unfortunately, I got a pretty good look at that 'road' on my way down into the valley. It doesn't exist anymore. Avalanche closed off the route."

Dirk spat a foul word. "We're in a box canyon. Trapped like rats."

Kent lifted his hands, palms out. "It's not a great situation, but it's not hopeless, either. When we don't arrive at our destination, searchers will look along the route of the flight plan we filed before we took off. Our current location is a little off that path, but not radically beyond reasonable range. One thing we can do is position chunks of glass on the stone chimneys of one or more of these buildings and along the cliff walls that will reflect the sunlight and hopefully draw the attention of airborne searchers. However, their search pattern will be lower than regular flight altitudes, so they are unlikely to fly through these mountains at night, which means we probably shouldn't bother with setting and tending bonfires after dark."

Lauren's mom let out a long gust of air. "At least we have a plan. Let's keep our hopes alive, people. And another thing we should do tomorrow is search this town top to bottom for anything we can use to make our time here easier, however short or long it may be."

"That's the pioneer spirit, Mom." Lauren exchanged a fist bump with her mother.

Kent smiled as ragged laughter erupted among most of the passengers, and the atmosphere lightened. Quite a pair of admirable women, these two.

Dirk's scowl barely dimmed. "The shorter the better." He tromped away to hunker down on one of the cushions near the heat source.

"I'm going to make one last trip out to the plane," Kent said. "Phil? Cliff? Are you still my main men?"

"What about me?" Dirk jumped up.

"I didn't think you'd want to handle luggage with a broken finger."

Dirk snickered. "You're right. I don't." He

turned his back and held out his hands toward the stove.

Kent gritted his teeth.

Cliff brushed past him with a sidelong look. "I'm about ready to smack the smirk off of Dirk."

Swallowing laughter, Kent followed him and big, lumbering Phil out the door. An hour later, as the sun closed in on the horizon, they returned with a full load of luggage and one stunning item that left all humor out in the cold.

Kent hauled Mags's wheelie and a bulky bundle into the makeshift hospital area. He stared down at his inert copilot, frost riming him from the inside out. Lauren took a look at his face and rose from her kneeling position.

"What is it?" she said. "And don't give me a slick answer."

Kent eyeballed the activity going on near the door where everyone was crowding around to receive their luggage. The prospect of jackets and additional clothing, as well as toiletry items, was exciting in a good way after all the excitement in a bad way. The thumping and bumping and babble of eager voices would likely cover any conversation between him and the too-insightful physician's assistant.

"This." He lifted the bulky pack. "It's a parachute."

Her eyes widened. "Isn't that standard equipment aboard your aircraft?"

He shook his head, bereft of speech as the possibilities—no, probabilities—buzzed around in his brain.

"Someone else brought it on board?"

"There is no tag on this item, so none of our passengers checked it in. Mags oversaw the loading of the luggage. She's the only one who could have put it there."

"But why?"

"That's the gazillion-dollar question, isn't it? Unfortunately, the answer stinks to the moon and back. Who would have needed an unorthodox exit from the aircraft?"

The sharp intake of Lauren's breath marked comprehension. "Only someone who knew an emergency was going to happen."

"Bingo. And the layout of my plane allows access to the luggage bay from the bathroom. Just sneak back there, don the chute and out you go. Nice and neat."

Color receded from her face. "So we have to conclude that the plane was sabotaged. Would

Mags have had the know-how to rig whatever caused the explosion?"

"Oh, yeah." Kent crossed his arms. "She was the bomb expert on our flight crew in Afghanistan."

"She was in the air force with you? Somebody you trusted? Wow. That's got to hurt."

Kent's skin tightened. She'd said a mouthful. It was hard to explain the camaraderie that developed between soldiers in the military. Such a level of betrayal bit deep, and somehow, this woman got it without explanation.

Lauren laid a hand on his arm. "We still don't know why she tried to destroy the plane."

"That, and which one of our passengers was in on the deal."

"What do you mean?" Her brows knit together.

He grimaced. "This is a tandem chute. Two people dive in it. Somebody was planning to leave with her, but got stuck in the plane with us because Mags was incapacitated."

Lauren's jaw dropped, and she leaned in toward him. "Someone walking around in this room tried to kill us? Wow. And they could try again!"

Kent delivered a single, decisive nod. "For now, let's keep the discovery of this parachute our secret. Her accomplice doesn't need to be alerted that his existence has been exposed."

"Allow him to relax, get complacent and maybe slip up somehow?"

"Exactly. And we need to pray that Mags wakes up—at least long enough to tell us his name—or we're all the proverbial sitting ducks. Anybody with the brains and guts to devise and carry out this sabotage plan will be quick to implement a Plan B that will glean him the same results—us dead and himself home free."

FOUR

A deep cough rent Lauren's chest, jerking her awake. A blanket wrapped around her where she lay against a hard floor, head cradled by a leather cushion. Acrid smoke gagged her nostrils and burned the back of her throat. She lunged to a sitting position, as hacking coughs and cries of "Fire!" converged from every direction.

Her mind spun. In front of her eyes, the room was dark as the inside of a barrel. From behind her shoulders, a ruddy heat cast a muted glow. Where was she? Oh, yes. The sabotaged plane. Emergency landing. Shelter in the abandoned mercantile. And now…fire!

Crash-bruised muscles protested her sudden scramble to get to her feet, but the blanket entangled her, and she fell backward hard on her behind. A moan and a cough came from her immediate right. Richard. No sound from her left. Mags remained unconscious...or worse.

"Help!" she cried through a strangled cough. "Help me with the patients."

Thumping noises, like hurried footsteps, answered her, but the sounds were headed in every direction except her location on the far side of the stove.

"Where's the door?" a male voice screamed. Cliff.

Yes, where was the door, but also, where was the fire? She glanced over her shoulders, and made out the dark form of the potbellied stove. All normal enough, and yet bitter, pine-tinged smoke swirled everywhere.

She had to get her patients out of here! Lauren yanked herself from the blanket's grip and stood, staring around. Hazy lights bobbed here and there. As they'd done before the group turned in last night, people were using their cell phone flashlights. Without cell service, the phones weren't good for much else, and from the volume of smoke in the room, not much good for lighting, either. The glow was more disorienting than illuminating.

"Where are you, Lauren?" Feminine tones rose above the panicked din.

"Mom!" Lauren answered. "Don't look—" she coughed "—for me! Find a way out!"

"Jade Eyes!"

A burn in the pit of Lauren's stomach joined the burn in her throat. Kent. She needed his strong arms and back to move Rich and Mags.

"Over here. Help me with the patients."

"Keep calling ou—" A throaty hack chopped off the last bit of the sentence.

"He…re!" Her lungs cramped against the invading fumes.

"Get low. Stay low, everyone." His voice was much closer and near her knees.

Lauren dropped down to join him. "Where?"

"Here." His hand found her arm.

"Grab… Rich. I'll…do my best…with Mags."

"I found it!" Phil's triumphal cry from the other end of the room announced the crash of the door flinging open and hitting the wall.

Chill air invaded the space, swirling the smoke, as the outdoor moonglow lit the atmosphere to fuzzy twilight. Even though smoke had to be escaping out the opening, the density around Lauren barely diminished. Smoke was being generated by something more quickly than it could disperse.

Watering eyes blurred her view of Kent's crouched figure grabbing Rich's shoulders and pulling him across the floor. Head spinning, Lauren struggled to focus and move Mags. Progress seemed almost nonexistent.

One foot. Two feet. Mags's inert body was as stubborn as an anchor against the rough and dusty floor. *Keep going. Got to keep going.* Lungs aflame, mouth dry as soot, Lauren forced flagging mind and muscles to labor on.

She must be getting close to the exit, yet the chill of the outdoor breeze seemed as far away as ever. Strange warmth clouded her brain. Inertia shrouded her muscles.

Crawling backward, tugging her patient, she ran into something solid behind her. What? A set of shelves. She'd set up her makeshift hospital with walls of moveable shelving units, which meant she wasn't even close to escape. She still had to pull her patient around the barrier. Nothing in her mind or body contained an ounce of ability to accomplish the impossible task. She wasn't going to make it.

But if she didn't make it, neither would Mags. The woman may have tried to kill them all, but she was a human being and Lauren's patient.

God, help us!

Her faint prayer seemed no more effective than a spurt of cool water against the overwhelming crush of hot darkness, yet a tiny surge of will brought her and her patient around the barrier. She stopped. She'd reached the end of herself. Lungs screaming, she slumped back on her heels, covering her mouth and nose with her arm and sleeve.

Consciousness ebbed. A murky shadow loomed over her, and then blackness fell. A funny sort of blackness, all soft and fuzzy. Strong arms hefted her. *Is that You, God, taking me home?* The room moved. No, *she* was moving. Cold embraced her. She came to rest on dusty ground, and smaller arms wrapped around her.

The sound of excited voices and deep coughs trickled into her consciousness, one voice very familiar. Her mother crooning to her, over and over. "It's okay, baby. Come back to me now."

Deep coughs racked Lauren's ribs, wrenching her insides. With a flailing arm, she flung the blanket from her head and hauled in a crisp, cold breath. Her head began to clear, but tears streamed from her eyes, clouding her vision. Vague figures, standing on the moon-washed street, appeared like swaying tree trunks.

"Be still, now, baby." Mom's arms tightened around her.

"I c-can't." Lauren pulled away, struggling to rise. Her dainty mother pulled her down, and Lauren had no strength to resist. "My patient…is in there!"

"Our hero pilot went to get her."

"Oh, no! Kent!"

"It's all right. He'll be all right."

"But—"

"If you must do something, dear, see to your other patient."

The Georgia peach voice contained a hint of sauce now, and Lauren choked on a laugh. How her incorrigible mother could draw a chuckle out of her in a situation like this was an amazement of nature. Lauren climbed to her feet and stood swaying and scrubbing at her eyes.

Where was he? Why wasn't someone helping?

Lauren stumbled forward, knocking against a figure that stepped into her path. The man cursed. Dirk. Who else! Lauren staggered around him, straining to see into the darkened doorway of the mercantile.

A strange-looking creature staggered out of the building onto the porch. Her clearing eyes finally sorted out the vision into a blanket-covered Kent carrying Mags's limp body in his arms. Phil clumped out of the small crowd and up the steps to support the swaying pilot.

The vise grip around Lauren's chest eased marginally. She made her way to the bottom step where Kent was laying out his copilot.

"There's no fire," Phil murmured as if to no one in particular, "just smoke."

Lauren knelt beside Kent and laid a hand on his spasming back as he coughed out the invading smoke from his lungs. His muscles rippled beneath her palm. Strong. Solid. Dependable. Lauren snatched her hand to herself as a memory surged to the fore. Her dad giving her four-year-old self a horsey ride on his strong, solid, dependable back. How she squealed and laughed and trusted that Daddies were forever. How deceiving appearances could be.

She shook her head, and pain shot through her oxygen-starved brain. No matter. She wasn't going to dredge up that old mess. Not now. Maybe not ever. She just needed to forget—stuff that memory back down in the dungeon where it belonged. Kent was nothing to her but a brave guy, excellent pilot and fearless leader for the moment. When they got out of this valley, he'd go his way, and she'd go hers. He was no threat to her hard-won equilibrium.

Time to turn to what was really important—her patients.

Lauren leaned in and placed two fingers against the carotid artery in Mags's neck. No pulse. She sucked air between her teeth and laid a hand against the woman's slack mouth.

No breath. She lowered her ear to the copilot's chest. No heartbeat.

"Ma…gs? Is sh-she…?" Kent's question came out ragged.

Lauren shook her head as she gazed up at Kent's cleanly sculpted features outlined by the moonlight. From his expression, she suspected more than strained lungs had caused the brokenness in his tone. The woman had been a comrade-in-arms at one time. What else might she have been to Kent before she tried to kill them? He'd never said.

"We could…try CPR," Lauren gasped out, "but I don't think…any of us has the breath… and I don't think…it would do any good. Her damaged brain…simply could not survive the lack of oxygen."

Their gazes locked and communicated. Now, Mags would never be able to tell them the identity of her accomplice. Did someone plan this strange, flameless fire? Who? How?

"Is everyone…else okay?" Kent called.

"Where's Neil?" Cliff's voice answered. "He never came out."

Heaving long breaths in and out of burning lungs, Kent climbed to his feet and squinted through watering eyes toward the mercantile. Smoke still poured through the open door like a chimney at Christmas, though maybe the volume had decreased slightly.

"If Neil is still in there," his words were leaden, "there is no point in going in after him until the fire in the stove goes out and the smoke lets up."

"What happened?" Dirk demanded. "Why are we driven out into the cold street in the middle of the night? This is unacceptable!"

"Would you care to speak with the concierge?" Phil rumbled.

A bout of snickers broke out, even as most of the group hugged themselves against the bitter wind.

"I would guess we have a plugged stovepipe," Kent said. "Not something we can fix until daylight. To stay warm, we'll have to climb into the transport wagon. We'll be packed like sardines, but our combined body heat will keep us from freezing."

"What about Mags's body?" Lauren inserted softly. "We heard coyotes howling when night fell. We can't leave her accessible to critters."

Kent grimaced. "The safest place for the moment would be on top of the wagon."

"But that would be pretty weird," Cliff said. "You know…hunkering down under—uh— well, a corpse."

"We're past being squeamish in this situation," Lauren's mother pronounced. "We will do what is right."

The velvet-gloved words generated action, at least from Cliff and Phil, as they assisted Kent in placing the blanket-wrapped body atop the wagon. Everyone's teeth were chattering by now, but Lauren insisted Rich be loaded inside first. His injured kneecap did not allow bending, so others would need to arrange themselves inside in a way to avoid the outstretched leg.

The man was barely conscious and moaned as they loaded him. "Waterrr!"

Kent gritted his teeth. The bottled water from the plane was inside the building, so the plea could not be answered until they could reenter the mercantile. His own throat rasped with every breath. Morning could not come soon enough.

But at last it did.

Groaning, Kent unwound himself from the tangle of people hunched inside the hearse-turned-tiny-house and stepped down onto the ground. In the overcast dawn, the weathered wooden buildings looked more forlorn than ever. Bird trills wove a lonely melody through the silence. The door to the mercantile stood open, no smoke rippling from the interior.

Lauren stepped out beside him, and long groans from within the wagon announced others rousing from whatever sleep-stupor they had managed to find after crowding inside.

"We'd better go in and look for Neil," she said.

Lips pressed together, Kent nodded. They walked in slow step onto the porch.

"Let me go first," he said.

She halted in compliance, and Kent stepped over the threshold into dim warmth. The smell of smoke combined with a tang of pine hung in the air, but no tendrils curled from the darkened stove. Nothing moved in the interior. Unsurprising. Who could have survived that much smoke inhalation? It was just a matter of locating Neil's bo—there! A huddled figure slumped on its side, facing the far wall.

Lauren's fingers closed around Kent's biceps. She must have seen him, too. Then she rushed ahead of him and knelt beside the still form. Kent caught up to her as she laid her fingers against his neck.

"What?" She snatched her fingers away as if burned and fixed a wide gaze up at him. "There's a pulse!"

The man groaned and lifted his head. Outdoor light showed through a small gap in the wall boards at floor level.

An invisible fist released its grip on Kent's lungs, and he barked a laugh. "You wily old curmudgeon!"

Neil coughed and shuddered as Lauren helped him sit up. Redness rimmed the man's eyes, his lips were cracked and his face was smudged with smoke and gray whisker stubble, but he was alive and breathing.

"Wily? Hardly, young man." He coughed. "More like the stupid chance of falling down in the dark and feeling a tiny breeze on my face. I snuggled up close to the wall and concentrated on taking my next breath. But I must have passed out. How did everyone else fare?"

Kent glanced at a tense-faced Lauren. She dropped her gaze.

"My copilot didn't make it," he said.

Neil lowered his head and huffed. "I'd hoped we'd all get out of this valley alive. What's the plan now?"

Noises from the other end of the mercantile brought their heads around. The bottled water was being ravaged by the thirsty travelers. Someone had even brought Rich inside and set him on the counter sideways with his injured leg up. He was gulping a drink as fast as he could.

"His color is better." Lauren smiled in Kent's direction. "If we can rig up some kind of crutch, he may even be able to get around a little."

Her smile sent a puff of warmth through his chest. Nothing to do with attraction, of course. Just glad to see someone with something to smile about. *Right? Right!*

"Hey, guys, Neil made it!" Cliff's near bellow turned attention to the amazing resurrection.

The elder executive received a round of backslaps, followed by a chorus of questions. In the melee, someone managed to pass Kent, Lauren and Neil bottles of water. Kent downed his practically in one gulp, and his throat felt less like the inside of a rusty pipe but tasted more like a pine tree from the hint of smoke that had seeped through the lid into the glass bottle. Perrier, of course. Nothing but the best in executive jets. Maybe the pine tang could be marketed. Kent swallowed his wry chuckle.

"Anything to eat around here?" Dirk's whine sliced into the celebration.

"Not much." Kent stuffed his hands in his jeans. "Whatever nuts and pretzels are left will have to be breakfast."

"What about lunch and dinner?" Dirk glared around at everyone.

"We're going to starve." Phil's words came out in a whispered wail.

"Not if I can help it," Kent said. "The great outdoors offers a variety of foods, even at this elevation, and I know what to look for. Haute cuisine, it will not be, but edible I can manage. We need to organize into pairs to explore the rest of this town and scavenge whatever we find useful. Rich can receive and organize whatever we scavenge, while Neil remains with him and restarts the fire in the stove once I clear out the pipe. Everyone is going to work together."

Kent settled a firm gaze on Dirk, who looked away, but said nothing.

"Aye-aye, Captain!" Neil saluted with a chuckle.

Cliff lifted a hand. "What about setting up those reflectors like you mentioned yesterday?"

Kent shook his head. "We *will* get to that later, but as long as the cloud cover remains low and thick like this, a reflector will have nothing to reflect. On the positive side, the clouds will drive a search plane low enough to eyeball the wreckage without any attention-getting devices."

"Yeah," grumbled Phil, "but they would have to fly directly over us. About like plopping straight onto the proverbial haystack needle."

"What else might we do to help ourselves be found?" Nina blinked up at Kent.

"Pray that the cloud cover lifts."

The older woman broke into a smile so like her daughter's. The two were definitely related, even though their appearances could hardly be more different.

"Excellent answer, young man."

Lauren looked up at him from examining Rich's leg. Her narrowed eyes and parted lips conveyed surprised assessment. Was faith a check in her positive column as it was in her mother's? He might be flirting with fire, but he'd be interested to hang around the tender-hearted, steel-willed PA long enough to find out. She intrigued him, and as long as he reined in the attraction, his heart would be fine.

The next half hour was dedicated to basic morning chores like trips behind the buildings for private needs, grabbing a light snack/breakfast and making good use of the small container of disinfectant wipes from the plane. Dirk and Cliff opted to shave. None of the other men bothered with their whiskers, especially after Neil made the comment that a little extra fur on the face might help keep them warm. They also moved Mags's body into the rear storage room of the mercantile.

Then Kent ordered everyone to layer up in well-smoked clothes from their suitcases and start organizing into pairs. Lauren's mom wanted to be with Lauren, but he nixed the idea of the two women going together.

"No offense," he said. "But we don't know what we might run into out there, and a guy's muscle might be a real asset."

"To compliment the feminine discernment of useful articles?" Nina lifted an elegant, teasing eyebrow.

"Exactly." Kent and the other men chuckled.

Even Lauren bit her lower lip against a laugh that her crinkled eyes betrayed.

"Very well. I shall go with Cliff." Nina linked her elbow with his. "And Dirk and Phil can be the other dynamic duo. Off we go then."

The foursome was on their way out the door before Kent could get his voice around words to stop them. That left him and Lauren to scavenge together. Not a good idea when he was doing his best to avoid any appearance of falling for the machinations of a matchmaking mama. He glanced at the young woman by his side. Her face had gone bright red, and she wasn't meeting his gaze.

A laugh escaped him. "Resourceful and quick, isn't she?"

"You don't know the half of it." The words sounded like they came from behind gritted teeth.

Apparently, Lauren was against her mother's high-handed antics as well. Should he be offended? Maybe he was. A little. Not because he had any romantic interest, of course, but on principle.

He cleared his throat. "Before we get started, I've got to go up on the roof and check out that stovepipe."

"There's a stairway up the back wall outside. Maybe you can reach the roof from there."

"Good idea."

Ten minutes later, Kent was scowling and yanking wads of pine branches out the top of the stovepipe. A far cry from the bird's nest he had expected. It was conceivable that a bird had nested on the edge of the chimney, and then the nest could have fallen into the hole because of vibrations due to using the stove. That, at least, would have been a natural phenomenon. This was not. He flung another fistful of well-toasted branches over his shoulder toward the edge of the roof.

"Hey, watch your throw."

Lauren's voice brought his head around. He'd left her at the top of the exterior stairs, but now she was standing on the flat roof with him. She was a strong, acrobatic woman.

"Sorry about that." Kent ran the fingers of one hand through his hair.

"Frustrated?"

"Spooked. And I don't mind admitting it. Fresh pine branches didn't stuff themselves down the chimney."

Color leached from her face. "Not an accident?"

"I wish."

Lauren hugged herself. "Someone tried to kill us again. They did kill Mags. We need to find out who it is."

"I'll add that to my to-do list." He reined in his bark on an exhale of breath. "Sorry. Not snapping at you, just—"

"Having a bellyful?"

"That would be an understatement. But speaking of bellies, we'd better get scavenging. First order of business is some kind of sizable container for pine cones. Pine nuts are nutritious."

"And delicious?"

"Depends on your taste buds." He shrugged. "You'll get your fiber and protein, though."

She laughed, and he managed a grin.

"There's a former blacksmith shop down the street," he said. "Looks like living quarters are on the second floor above it. Maybe we'll find tools or a few containers and utensils there. Especially a usable bucket. We need to transport water. We also need a shovel or two for...well, for lots of things."

"Like digging a grave?"

Kent pressed his lips together and nodded. "We will have some sort of funeral as soon as possible, whether we have a shovel or not. If nothing else, we should be able to find plenty of rocks to serve as a makeshift crypt."

Lauren turned away with a sober nod. Kent took her hand and helped lower her off the side of the roof onto the stair landing below. Unlike her mother, she wasn't dainty in her height or build. She was solid and sturdy, but feminine, and her hand was slender and soft in his big, rough one. His heart rate sped up.

What were the chances that he would somehow be able to get her to safety and civilization? He didn't dare give that question long attention, or he'd never be able to keep up a strong front for the group in his care. Truth be told? He was scared spitless. Their chances of rescue, much less survival, were so very slim—even without the specter of a mysterious killer looming over them. But fear wasn't going to cut it. Not if he wanted any hope of ensuring the world didn't lose the services of this compassionate and courageous woman.

Lauren took her hand back as soon as they reached the landing, leaving Kent's with an odd emptiness. Face pale and grim, she stuffed her hands into the pockets of the light jacket she wore over her layers of clothing.

"I'll follow your lead to the blacksmith shop," she said.

On the way up the street, she was quiet, gnawing on her lower lip. Her thoughts about their situation were probably as grim as his.

They arrived at a building open to the air on three sides. The high, first-floor ceiling was topped by a fully enclosed second story. Untidy remains of an abandoned business rested in the shade of the upper floor—an anvil, a long-cold furnace, the rusty frame of a wagon wheel, and some kind of industrial-sized rake about four feet by six feet with rows of rusty tines that might have been dragged by a mule or horse to level taconite mounds. No useful equipment, not even a hammer.

Kent sighed, and Lauren echoed him.

"Let's go upstairs." He led the way cautiously up a rickety set of wooden steps on the side of the structure.

Unsurprisingly, other than a weary creak,

the ancient door managed no resistance to their intrusion. A musty, rodent-like smell greeted their entrance, but no critters jumped and ran. Any sustenance for them here was probably long exhausted.

Lauren sneezed as dust swirled up around their feet. Dirty windows allowed enough light to make out a mostly empty room that might have been a kitchen, judging by the stovepipe sans stove that poked out of one wall. A cupboard beckoned on the opposite wall, and a table, hosting a few objects unidentifiable in the dimness, leaned against the far wall.

"I'll take the cupboard, if you want to see what's over there." He gestured toward the table. "Just be careful where you step. We don't know—"

A splintering crack halted him, and he whirled to find Lauren windmilling for balance on the lip of a hole that had opened in the floor. She lost her battle to pull back from the edge even as Kent let out a strangled cry and lunged for her.

FIVE

Every muscle in Lauren's body fought to remain upright, but gravity sucked her into the black hole beneath her feet. Her throat slammed closed as she went airborne.

A steely hand wrapped around her wrist and jerked her plummet to a halt. Pain shot up her arm and shoulder. Reflexively, her free hand grabbed Kent's arm, and she dangled, swaying back and forth like a metronome.

"Hang on, Jade Eyes," he said. "I'll pull you up."

Air finally slipped through her constricted throat into her lungs, and she lifted her gaze to his. "Maybe it would be better for you to just lower me. I can't be far from the floor below now."

"I don't think that's a good idea. Keep your eyes on me, and don't look down."

She looked and let out a thin shriek. Less than a foot beneath her, the rusty tines of the industrial rake stabbed upward. If she had hit the floor, forget worries about a broken bone. She would have been impaled like a shish kebab. Probably dead instantly.

Her fingers convulsed around Kent's wrist as he drew her slowly upward. Soon she was able to help pull herself onto the floorboards of the second story. Quivering in every limb, she burrowed into Kent's strong embrace, and they huddled together in the dust.

"I can't believe…that was so…" Her scrambled brain couldn't put into words what she felt. Her heart hammered against her ribs like a panicked bird in a cage. "Thank you…I could have been…"

"It's all right. You're okay now." Kent's warm breath flowed over her ear where her head was tucked into the curve of his shoulder.

Reluctantly, she pulled back and met his gaze. If she didn't know better, the stoic pilot's world had been rocked. His eyelids blinked rapidly, and a suspicion of moisture filmed his eyes.

She blinked back wetness in her own eyes. "My fault. I wasn't as careful as I should have been. At least, this is just a near-accident, not a deliberate death trap."

"I'm not ready to draw that conclusion without further investigation."

"But how could someone from our party have set up a trap like this overnight?"

Kent's shoulders rolled in a shrug. "How did the culprit gather pine boughs and stuff them into the stovepipe on the mercantile roof last night in the dark? But someone did."

Lauren climbed to her feet, and Kent did the same. Keeping her gaze lowered, she slapped dust from her jeans and jacket. If she looked at him, her eyes might betray her sudden silly desire to be wrapped in his arms again. What was wrong with her? The danger was over. Time to stand on her own two feet again.

"Maybe someone else lives in this burg," she said.

"How likely is it that a secret resident of this abandoned town is trying to kill us at the same time as a saboteur downed our plane? Besides, we've seen no sign of habitation. Two deadly assassins in Trouble Creek is beyond credible."

"So is the fact that we're here at all."

"I'll give you that." Kent barked a laugh. "Someone crept out of the mercantile last night, probably through the storage room in the back and on into the alley. That someone must have used the flashlight on their phone to pick their way around. We should be looking for someone whose battery is about to give out."

"You're thinking like a sleuth now." She released a weak chuckle. "My turn. Rich isn't a suspect because he can't get around on his own. And I might even exclude Neil because of his age, but he's awfully spry."

"That leaves us with Phil, Cliff, Dirk and your mother. But I'm excluding your mom, not because she isn't physically capable, but because I can't wrap my head around her trying to kill you."

Lauren scowled. "Don't even go there on a maybe. And not just because I'm her daughter. My mom can hardly kill a spider, and she hates those. Besides, what motive would she have?"

"What motive does anyone in our party have? That's an important question we need to answer." He turned away and bent over the hole Lauren had nearly fallen through. "Doesn't look like the flooring was tampered with by anything except rodent teeth and rot. Let's go below and check around that rake for any footprints in the dust. If the rake was moved, foot size might give us a hint at identity."

A minute later, Lauren massaged the strained

muscles of her shoulder as she frowned at the evidence. No clear footprints, just a few scuffs, but drag marks in the dirt floor showed the rake had been deliberately positioned, tines up, beneath the faulty flooring.

"Look at this." Kent shone the light of his cell up at the boards above. "The cracks and weak areas in the floorboards are visible to the naked eye when illuminated."

Lauren snorted. "It would have been simple and quick to set up this trap. I wonder what other traps might be waiting for us. Oh, no!" Lauren grabbed Kent's bicep. "My mother! What if she's alone with the saboteur? What about the others? We have to warn them—"

A masculine yowl split the thin mountain air, followed by a crash.

"Sounds like that came from the mercantile." He took off toward the store.

Stomach roiling, Lauren stuck to his heels. What catastrophe now? They burst into the building to find Neil trying to help Rich sit up from a sprawl atop a set of flattened shelving.

Lauren rushed to him. "Are you okay? What happened?"

Red-faced, Rich shook his head. "Nothing more injured than my pride. I was trying to hop around a little and lost my balance."

A long breath gushed from Lauren's chest,

echoed by Kent who was standing over them. Footfalls sounded on the porch boards.

"What's going on?"

"Everyone all right?"

The alarmed questions shot from Phil and Dirk as they plunged into the building, huffing and puffing. Their shoulders slumped as they received the explanation and relief hit.

Neil's nubbin whiskers rasped as he ran a hand over his face. "I don't know if I can take any more excitement."

"How goes the scavenging?" Kent asked.

Phil shook his head. "The townspeople really cleaned the place out when they left."

Kent frowned. "We need to keep looking, but folks, be careful out there." He glanced toward Lauren, gaze grim.

She nodded. They had to tell people about the sabotaged stovepipe and the trap at the blacksmith's, even if suspicion toward one another would infect them like a plague and escalate a critical situation to the point of unbearable. But everyone had a right to know they harbored a killer among them, and they needed to be on their guard against more than their challenging natural surroundings. Some of their party was missing at this very moment. Lauren's heart clenched.

"Where are my mom and Cliff? Surely, they would have heard the commotion, too, and come running."

"We'll search for them as soon as I've given the rest our news," Kent said.

"News?" Neil's eyebrows climbed.

"You two engaged or something?" Dirk displayed a nasty grin.

Heat crept up Lauren's neck and onto her cheeks. "He means important information." The words came out between gritted teeth.

God forgive her, but slapping that sneer off the obnoxious executive's face was an appealing option. She took a deep breath and reined in her impulses.

All eyes fixed on Kent, whose face had taken on the chiseled quality of someone tasked with an awful but unavoidable chore.

"Our stovepipe was deliberately stuffed with pine boughs, and a few minutes ago, Lauren narrowly escaped death from a purposely laid trap. Someone among us is—"

Excited conversation and footsteps on the porch halted Kent's stark explanation. At the sound of her mom's voice, Lauren's heart lightened.

Her mother and Cliff entered the store, grinning like conquerors and holding aloft their prizes. Mom held a steel-handled broom in one hand and a large plastic bucket in the other. Cliff hefted a shiny hatchet and a shovel. The very modern items could not have originated in the nineteenth century. They could only have come from this one.

"Proof!" Mom proclaimed. "We are not alone in Trouble Creek."

Kent's mind raced. Not alone? Someone actually lived in this ghost town? That changed everything he'd been assuming.

Maybe none of the passengers were involved in the deadly traps. And what if he was wrong about one of them being involved in the sabotage of his plane? But that didn't make sense. Who had been intended as the second jumper for the tandem parachute? Or had he leaped to a false conclusion about his copilot? Maybe the parachute had been present in the cargo bay for some innocent reason. Then who sabotaged the plane? It had to have been someone with access and an understanding of planes and a working knowledge of bomb-making. Or was he mistaken about the cause of their crash landing? Maybe there was a natural explanation.

No! He couldn't make any natural scenario add up, but examining his plane for concrete evidence of tampering just shot to the top of his to-do list—right up there with uncovering the faceless enemy who was trying to kill them in a supposedly abandoned mining town.

"Where did you get those things?" Kent's question sliced through the stunned silence.

Still smiling like the canary-getting cat, Lauren's mom set the bucket on the stationary counter. "There's a one-room hut on the far side of the town near the cliffs. It looks as shabby on the outside as any of the other buildings, but the inside is fixed up. There's a bed and a stove and a table that could be original with the town, but then there are other things that could only come from a store in our day and age."

"Was there any food?" Phil rubbed his pudgy hands together.

"Canned goods and jerky," Cliff said. "A few other things."

"What are we waiting for?" Dirk headed for the door, leading a small stampede of the other men.

Lauren made no move to follow but turned a shadowed gaze on Kent.

"Hold it!" He gave free rein to his air force captain voice, and everyone froze, staring at him. "We're not going to run down there and loot the place."

Neil narrowed his eyes. "But this is an emergency situation. Surely, it can be justi-fied—"

"More emergency than you realize," Lauren inserted. "Whoever lives in that cabin may be trying to kill us."

"Kill us?" Lauren's mother echoed faintly. "What do you mean?"

Kent repeated what he'd told the others about the pine boughs in the stovepipe and the trap that nearly took Lauren's life. Nina squeaked and hugged her daughter.

The older woman turned a tear-stained face toward Kent. "And to think I left the person a sweet thank-you note on the table with a promise to pay for anything we used or con-sumed."

"You are a true lady, Mrs. Barrington," Kent said. "But even more important than food and manners, did you see any kind of device that could communicate with the out-side world?"

Cliff shook his head. "Just the pen and paper Nina used to write the thank-you note."

A collective groan left the throats of the survivors.

Kent held up a calming hand. "Clearly, our

lone resident of Trouble Creek gets supplies from the world at large from time to time, so there must be a way out of this valley that leads to civilization. We need to talk to this person, but we have to approach with caution. So far, the attempts on our lives have taken the form of booby traps, but since the need to hunt game is almost a given up here, the person probably has a gun."

"We may be dealing with someone who is mentally unbalanced," Lauren added, "so we can't count on rational or predictable behavior."

"Or maybe a crook who is hiding from the law," Nina said with a nod.

Kent pursed his lips. "In that case, our mystery resident would be desperate to keep his location secret. Absolutely no one should go anywhere alone from now on."

"What you're saying is we're not safe anywhere." Hysteria edged Dirk's tone. "I'm not going outside again."

Cliff snorted. "What's to stop him from barging in here and letting us have it? It's not like we have any way to defend ourselves."

Kent turned away and headed for his duffel. He'd left it atop the cushion he used to cradle his head at night. "Our best hope for survival, much less safety, is to get out of this valley."

He unzipped his bag, shoved aside a pile of clothing and the binoculars he regularly took with him, and pulled out his Beretta M9 and a box of cartridges.

"I'm sticking with *him* everywhere he goes," Dirk proclaimed.

"How good are you with that thing?" Neil asked.

Kent stood up, Beretta dangling by his side. "Good enough to plink a rabbit if one pops up within range…or seriously discourage someone who starts shooting at us."

Neil's eyes narrowed. "With your survival knowledge, you're more than just a flyboy."

Kent shot the older man a wolfish grin. "Born and raised in the Florida everglades. Rough-and-tumble fourth son in a family of eight. We boys would spend days in the wild, living off the land. As for other environments, the air force trained me in SERE."

"SERE?" Lauren asked.

"Survival, Evasion, Resistance and Escape."

"Perrrfect!" Nina clapped her hands together. "If we must be stranded in a hostile environment, the good Lord has placed us in the right hands."

Dirk sniffed. "Yeah, well, if the good Lord was so good at planning, why are we stuck here at all?"

"Oh, shut it, DJ." Phil scowled.

"You shut it. I'm not going to take any of your—"

"Enough!" Kent strode toward the door. "Dirk, Cliff, Lauren, come with me." He stopped at the threshold. "We'll go to this cabin and get some food and cooking utensils, hopefully even some kerosene for the lanterns. Phil and Neil, go to the stream with that bucket and bring us back some water. Nina and Rich, stay here. Close the door after us. If you sense any threat, take cover behind the stationary counter until we return."

Phil crossed his arms and stuck out a full lower lip. "What if this desperate criminal shoots us at the stream?"

"If our mystery resident is watching us, he's far more likely to try to defend his home than take potshots at water carriers. If anything, I figure we'll draw him our way."

"Then Lauren is *not* going with you." Nina grabbed her daughter's arm.

"Lauren is definitely going." She disengaged from her mother's grip and headed toward Kent.

Something warm flowered in his heart at the trust in her gaze. In her value system, trust seemed to be a precious resource— hard-earned and easily lost. Something had scarred her deeply. She hadn't opened up to him enough for him to see what it was, but at least she had confidence in him to protect her life. What might it be like if one day she trusted him with more than her physical life? And what was it about this woman that made him crave to find out—even against his better judgment and bitter experience?

Kent turned and walked out the door. If he didn't succeed in keeping her alive, he'd never know. *Keep your head in the game, Garland.*

Mentally kicking himself, he tucked the Beretta into the waistband of his jeans and led the way up the dusty main street of Trouble Creek. As he walked, his gaze scanned every nook and cranny for a concealed figure. Truth be told, if this guy—assuming the hostile resident was male—wanted to stay hidden, he would be hard to find. Or if he had a rifle, a handgun would be poor defense against potshots raining down on them from the cliffs.

Kent's gaze scanned the high rock walls that hemmed them in. The scree-covered slopes rose gradually at first and then sharply for the last hundred yards or so. Where were the mine entrances? Had they been blasted closed before the miners left? Under the overcast sky, it was difficult to make out details on the rock faces.

"Okay, we're at the edge of town, Cliff. Where is this inhabited cabin?"

The man guided them past the final main street building—a former saloon, judging by the batwing doors hanging on rusty hinges—and veered to the left. Beyond the protection of the buildings, a sudden gust of wind kicked up dust devils, peppering his face with dirt granules.

A sharp sneeze announced Lauren coming up beside him. He offered her a small smile. Her answering smile was faint as her eyes kept performing a dance similar to his, scanning terrain and surroundings. She would have made an excellent soldier. Her spot-on instincts and reflexes continually amazed him—except when she was engaged in trying to save someone's life. Then she seemed to care less about herself and did things like staying too long in a smoke-filled building or unbuckling her seat belt to help someone during a flight emergency.

"There it is!" Cliff pointed.

The cabin sat on the outskirts of a cluster of long, low structures that might have been bunkhouses for the miners. It was squat and square and, except for the unbroken windows, appeared in about the same state of neglect as the bunkhouses.

"Wait here," Kent said to the others while he approached the hut.

As he stepped onto the low stoop, the back of his neck prickled. He moved to the side of the door, opened it with one hand and waited for a bullet that might welcome an intruder. None come, and no sound wafted out from within. The cabin might be as deserted as it had been when Cliff and Nina had been there, but now was not a time to take chances.

He darted inside, eyes and gun swiveling in the practiced arc his training had taught him. Bed: wider than a single but narrower than full and neatly made up. Table: small and rough-hewn but sturdy. Stove: wood or coal burning with two-burner range. Floor-to-ceiling shelf: home to canned goods, boxed crackers, sacks of sugar and flour, common spices and plastic containers labeled "jerky" and "trail mix" respectively, as well as other food supplies.

No human being. No guns or weapons of any kind, which was a little strange in itself. In fact, no sign of recent habitation. Everything was coated in dust. No one had been here within the last few weeks. The report of a psycho inhabitant of Trouble Creek had been greatly exaggerated—somewhat by their own fears, but mostly through lack of information.

Now, as far as he was concerned, they were back to square one: suspecting each other as a killer in their midst. A far more troubling problem.

"All clear," he called to the others.

Lauren trooped in first and looked around. She swiped a finger of dust from the tabletop. "Hey, no one has been here in a while."

"I know." Kent shook his head.

She huffed. "Apparently, Mom forgot that little detail."

"I did, too," Cliff admitted as he stepped inside. "Guess I was so excited about finding food and stuff we can use that I didn't even think about the undisturbed dust."

"All right then," Kent said. "No harm done. Let's gather up whatever we can use, and—"

"How about, instead, Mom and I move in here," Lauren said. "The rest of you can set up housekeeping in one of those bunkhouses?"

Kent issued a good-natured, mock bow. "The lady has a fine idea."

"I thought you might see it my way. Particularly since we can cook everyone a decent meal as soon as we get some water."

Dirk let out an enthusiastic cheer. "Finally, some small semblance of civilization. Now we just need—"

A hideous wail chopped through the

thought. The hairs on Kent's arms rose to attention. The sound didn't come from inside the town. It came from the direction of the creek. The wail rose higher and higher, and a second scream joined the first. Neil and Phil were in trouble. He'd heard such screams before. In Afghanistan. In Iraq.

Please, God, don't let it signal the kind of horror I've hoped never to see again.

SIX

Lauren's feet took wings before her brain kicked into gear. What was she thinking, running toward the danger? But she couldn't stop. People were hurt. A figure darted into her path, and she slammed into a broad chest. The impact staggered her backward, but didn't move Kent an inch.

"What are you doing?" She glared up at him. "I have to help."

"Not without some serious recon first, and I'm the best equipped for that assignment. Cliff, Dirk, head back to the mercantile and barricade the doors as best you can."

The men trotted off, darting spooked glances in every direction. The screams had ceased, and Lauren's skin prickled in the eerie silence.

"You're letting me come with you?"

A wry grin tugged at one corner of Kent's mouth. "Other than hog-tying you, I'm not sure how I'd stop you. But keep behind me, and do exactly what I say."

"Agreed."

Drawing the handgun from his waistband, he set off at a lope. Lauren stayed on his heels as they crossed the main street at an angle, darted between buildings and entered a tiny residential area of small, clapboard houses. Dry grass crunching beneath their feet, Kent led them between a pair of the structures. He stopped at the far corner of one building and pressed himself against the wall. Lauren copied his movements.

Here, the burble of the creek about a hundred yards distant was softly audible, but the water was hidden beyond a gentle rise crowned by a stand of pine trees. No human voices or outcries carried on the wind, and no one was in view. Lauren's chest tightened. What had happened to Neil and Phil?

Kent looked over his shoulder at her, face set and grim. "There isn't much cover between here and the creek, but we heard no gunshots, so hopefully, we're not dealing with a marksman—unless it's a pro with a silencer."

"How weird would that be in this abandoned town?"

"Unfortunately, there's a whole lot of weird going on around here. But I'm going to chance it, and take off for the creek. You stay put and watch me."

Lauren opened her mouth to protest, but he lifted a forestalling hand. "No argument. If I go down, then you hustle back to the others in the mercantile."

"And then what?" She planted her hands on her hips. "Wait for the assassin to come finish us before we starve? Without you, we're all as good as dead."

Kent turned and gripped her shoulder. "Don't think like that. Think rescue. We've got to believe help is coming. Just...stay alive!"

The fire in his gaze scorched straight to her heart, and she nodded. Jaw clenched, she watched him race across the open expanse of grassy hummocks and taconite scree. Then he disappeared beyond the rise into the creek basin.

Lauren's heart hammered in her ears. What was he finding by the creek? Her imagination conjured images of blood and death, but she squashed the useless speculation. A long minute ticked past. Her feet itched to move— to do anything but stand in the shadows. The walls of the two houses seemed to be closing in on her. Even the dreary sky seemed to be pressing down on her head.

"Lauren! I've found them. Come quickly!"

Her heart leaped at Kent's yell, rendered faint by distance. She started to step forward, but the world went dark as a nasty-smelling blanket settled over her head, followed by a pair of powerful arms girdling her trunk and clamping her arms against her sides. A yelp left her throat, muffled by the rough cloth. The arms squeezed with the strength of a bear. She couldn't fit a breath in her lungs. Her ribs creaked.

This is it, God? I'm going to be squeezed to death by a human python?

Not without a fight, she wasn't. She struggled and kicked, but her attacker lifted her feet off the ground, slammed her to the earth facedown, and landed on top of her. This guy wasn't just a bear; he was a moose. Her whole body was covered by his. She couldn't move more than a pinky finger. Bile choked her. Dizziness swamped her brain.

Garbled words rasped in her ear, but she couldn't make out their meaning.

"Wha-wha—?" she croaked, not managing to make any more sense than her assailant.

The man let out more guttural noises that strove to form into words, but came short.

"Lauren?… Lauren?" Kent's voice sounded nearer each time he spoke her name.

The weight suddenly lifted off her, and heavy footfalls faded in retreat. Lauren lay frozen, breathing in ragged gasps. She had to get this stinking blanket off her head, but her trembling limbs refused to cooperate.

"Lauren!"

Kent was here. His voice shot life into her, and she struggled to her knees, flailing against her shroud. Then it was gone—plucked from her—and the smoky pine scent of Kent's clothing filled her nostrils as he knelt with her, and she buried her head in his shoulder. They seemed to be making a habit of this position, but it was a nice habit. One she could get used to.

"What happened?" He stroked her hair, and a pleasurable shiver ran through her. "Are you hurt?"

"I'm fine. It was him! The mystery dweller."

Kent pressed her away from him. Oh, how she wanted to cling, but she didn't. Her arms fell to her sides.

"Which way did he go?" Kent's gaze looked beyond her.

Limp and weak, Lauren motioned back the way they had come between the two houses.

"I have to see if I can catch him." Kent leaped to his feet. "Head for the creek. You're needed there."

Then he was gone. A familiar ache spread from her core into every extremity. *Abandoned again.* Stupid thought, but emotions weren't rational. Of course, Kent had to go after the guy that was a danger to them all. It was unreasonable of her to expect him to stay by her side. She was a big girl. Yes, she was.

Lauren struggled to her feet, knees wobbly. Leaning against the wall beside her, she drew in deep breaths and let them out slowly. The blanket that her attacker had used lay crumpled against the foundation of the other house. It appeared to be made of some rough, rust-red-and-dirty-white-striped cloth. Probably a horse blanket, if the sweaty animal smell was any indication. It wasn't all that large, but it was thick. Probably why she'd had difficulty breathing with it over her head.

Had the guy intended to kill her? Smother her to death or maybe dispatch her with a knife or some other weapon? There had been no indication of a weapon in the brief encounter, but that didn't mean her attacker hadn't been armed with more than a blanket. Then again, maybe he'd only wanted to talk to her. Funny way to begin a conversation. Besides, the guy seemed to have problems communicating. A speech impediment? Or maybe her attacker's objective was to frighten her out of her mind. In that, he'd succeeded. But why? What had he hoped to accomplish?

Lauren began moving toward the creek, slowly, then faster and faster. She was needed. That was what Kent had said. She could share her thoughts about the attack with him when they were together again. Provided the hostile inhabitant of Trouble Creek didn't hurt him. Not likely. Kent Garland was a force to be reckoned with. He'd proven that much. Besides, she needed him to be okay. No, they all needed him to be okay. There was nothing personal about her concern for his safety. Nothing personal at all.

Sure, and the sun rises in the west, a little voice taunted in her head. She told it to hush up as she half walked, half slid down an embankment to the edge of the creek below.

"Neil? Phil?" she called.

"We're over here!" Neil's cry sent her upstream toward a bend in the water that disappeared around a clump of pines.

Lauren hurried on, hopping over and around rocks dotting the bank. Here, the creek was about twenty feet across and sparkling clear straight to its stony bottom, except in a darker middle section maybe six feet wide where a fast current must have dug a deeper trench.

She rounded the bend and stopped short. Ahead lay a wooden dam with a wide pond beyond it. The work of beavers? Made sense in this mountain wilderness. Considerable water spilled over the dam, but it held firm. She'd read somewhere that beavers built strong and to last.

Movement caught her eye. There, by the bank of the pond, a pair of figures huddled— one wiry, the other doughy. One of Phil's legs was stretched out straight, and the foot disappeared into the water. He clutched the thigh of that leg with both hands. His moans carried to her as she drew closer. Both faces gazed up at her as if her very presence might instantly deliver them from whatever problem they faced. Phil's was puffy and moist with tears or sweat or both, mouth twisted in a fixed grimace. Neil's was white and strained, mouth pressed into a thin line.

"What seems to be the prob—" Her words halted as her gaze found Phil's submerged foot.

The clear water did nothing to hide the chain that held him fast by metal jaws clamped around his foot.

She gulped. "You've stepped in a trap, and I have no clue how to get you free."

Kent stomped back toward the crisis at the stream. Whoever attacked Lauren was surely flesh and blood, but as for finding him, the guy might as well be made of smoke. Of course, the "mystery dweller," as Lauren had called him, knew this whole valley better than anyone. He could have a dozen hidey-holes. Their crash landing into his domain must have driven him into one of them.

But why did the dust in the cabin testify that he hadn't lived there for a while? And why was he so fearful of them that he would start booby-trapping the place? Assuming, of course, that he was behind the stuffed stovepipe, the deadly rake setup, and now the beaver trap clamped on Phil's foot. His mind found the man's guilt a logical conclusion, but his gut begged to differ.

Something didn't add up. Correction—lots of somethings didn't add up. He was in a mood to start demanding answers, beginning with his motley array of passengers. It would suit him fine if Dirk the conniving jerk was the one in on sabotaging his plane, but sandpaper personality didn't automatically make a person a heartless killer. Motive was the key, but how did he uncover the reason for downing the plane?

Excited voices up ahead alerted him that he was about to rejoin Phil, Neil and Lauren. Kent hurried his steps. He'd failed to catch the man who'd attacked Lauren and might be trying to kill them with his deadly tricks. Now, priority one was Phil.

"There you are!" Lauren exclaimed as he rounded the bend in the stream. "Did you catch him?"

Her gaze searched his, but he delivered a small shake of the head.

Her shoulders drooped. "Would you happen to have a clue how to get Phil out of this thing? I can't treat him until we do. We need to hurry. He's going into shock."

The big man was deathly pale and shaking like an aspen leaf. Lauren had taken off her jacket and put it across Phil's lap. Neil had done the same, and all three were shivering. He might as well join the party. Kent slipped out of his jacket and draped it around Phil's shoulders.

"Th-thank you," Phil muttered through chattering teeth. "I'm sorry to be such a k-klutz. I stepped out onto a rock as I was scooping up the water, but my f-foot slipped and this…this *thing* snapped onto m-me."

"Are you in pain?" Kent asked.

"Not now. Most of my leg is n-numb."

"Be thankful for that," Lauren said. "And that this trap doesn't have teeth. You could be bleeding to death."

"Small mercies, eh?" Neil stuffed his hands in his pockets.

Kent knelt and began undoing the heavy-duty laces on his hiking boots. He'd changed into those and some jeans as soon as they'd retrieved their luggage yesterday.

"What are you doing?" Impatience seeped through Lauren's tone.

"This is a Conibear trap."

"A bear trap!" Neil burst out. "There are bears around here?" The man's wide gaze darted here and there.

"Not a *bear* trap. A Conibear trap. Commonly used for small animals like beavers and muskrats. The jaws snap closed with ninety pounds of pressure, so—"

"We're likely dealing with a broken foot," Lauren finished his sentence.

"Almost certainly." Kent finished pulling his laces from his shoes. "But if it had been a steel bear trap with those big teeth, we would likely be dealing with a shattered leg and major blood loss, possibly even an amputation."

"So I should count my b-blessings?" Phil's

eyes went wide then his pupils rolled back in his head, and he slumped sideways onto the ground.

Lauren knelt beside her patient. "Can't you and Neil pull those jaws open? Hurry!"

"Human strength won't open the trap. It takes a surprising little tool." Kent kicked off the laceless boots and pulled off his socks.

She gaped at him as he waded barefoot into the water and crouched over the trap. He'd thought he was cold a moment ago, but the icy current swirling around his calves sent deep shivers to his core. He ignored the discomfort as he tied one shoestring to the top loop of the spring, ran the string through the bottom spring loop and back through the top spring loop. Rising, he stood on the trap chain, pinning the trap to the bottom of the stream, and hauled up on the string with all his might. Slowly, both sides of the trap spring met. He tied off the shoestring and repeated the process on the other side of the trap.

"He's free."

"That's amazing!" Neil burst out.

"Help me pull him away from the water."

As soon as they got the big man up the bank, Lauren gently removed Phil's loafer. Kent grimaced. Even through the man's black sock, a deep indentation in the crown of the foot was clear and pronounced.

"The foot has been crushed," Lauren said. "The precise extent of the damage will be difficult to assess without X-rays. But shock is the biggest threat right now. Any treatment to the injury will have to wait until we get him someplace warm."

"We all need to get warm." Neil hugged himself.

"Before I headed back here," Kent said, "I stopped at the mercantile, told the rest about your encounter with the mystery dweller and asked them to bring up the wagon for Phil. If I'm not mistaken, that's them now."

A rattling noise grew louder, along with the sound of human voices. Many hands helped load Phil into the wagon, and soon they were all back in the relative warmth of the mercantile. Lauren oversaw arranging her new patient on cushions with his foot elevated and making sure every available blanket was piled onto him. The man was groaning and coming around to consciousness when Kent slipped into the back room to change into dry pants.

The sight of Mags's blanket-wrapped body shot a pang through him. They had a shovel now. She could be laid to rest—at least temporarily until they got out of this valley. If that didn't happen soon, they would be digging more graves. And if they never got out, who would dig that last one? The mystery dweller?

Lauren's strong, lovely face appeared before his mind's eye and reined in Kent's thoughts. *Morbid much, Garland?*

While Lauren continued to work over her now conscious patient, Kent grabbed the shovel and let everyone know what he was going to do. Somber nods greeted the announcement.

"Want help?" Cliff asked.

"I can handle this alone. I want to, actually."

Lauren emerged from her makeshift hospital, rubbing her hands. "What about the mystery dweller?"

"I'm the one with the gun. I'll be fine. Cliff, you and Dirk make a quick trip to the old cabin. Fetch the container of jerky and a cookpot to sterilize the water Neil remembered to bring back from the stream. Maybe some of those canned goods, too. I think I spotted a container of kerosene. Don't forget that item. The idea of the women moving into that cabin isn't going to fly with the threat of the mystery dweller confirmed. We need to stay together here, but we can't hide indoors every minute. Everyone needs food and safe drinking water ASAP. I can testify I'm starving, and I haven't even dug that grave yet."

Rumbles of assent greeted Kent's summary of the situation.

"I'll stay here and watch over the ladies and the patients," Neil said. "Any chance you have an extra pistol?"

"Sorry."

Neil shrugged. "Just thought I'd ask."

Kent threw him a casual salute as he headed out to perform his sad chore. The best spot he could think of was right next to the plane wreckage. Critters might be less likely to dig where the smell of humans abounded. Besides, it was past time to get a good look at the damage under the belly of the plane.

The body of the jet took the edge off the chill wind as his shovel bit into the ground. The earth was hard-packed but not frozen. Yet. By the time his trench was a foot deep, sweat trickled down his chest under his layers of shirts and jacket. He persevered until he had a rectangle about four feet deep.

The crunch of footsteps brought his head around and sent one hand to the butt of his pistol. Lauren lifted her arms in mock surrender. Kent relaxed and took his hand off the gun. With his jacket sleeve, he rubbed the sweat off his forehead.

"Under the circumstances, we all need to

get in the habit of calling out when we approach someone."

"You're right." Her color heightened. "Sorry."

"What made you come out here alone?"

Her chin lifted as a flash of jade eyes telegraphed irritation. "I didn't figure an assailant would be able to come at me out in the open like this, and if he has a gun, having someone with me would only put that person in danger, too."

"Fair enough. Doesn't mean I like any of us traipsing around alone."

"Except you?"

"I've got my equalizer with me." He grinned.

She scowled. "We need to talk."

"I'm on it with both ears."

"Will you kindly stop being aggravating and take me seriously?"

He stifled a chuckle. Should he tell her he was doing it on purpose so he could see those eyes flash? Not if he valued his life. What was the matter with him? Was he flirting with this woman? The thought sobered him immediately.

"I *am* taking you and this whole situation very seriously, but the tighter the spot the more soldiers—even ex-soldiers—default to humor."

Her expression relaxed. "I've heard that

about people in other high-risk occupations, like police officers and firefighters. Believe it or not, nurses and docs can get a little nuts with the medical humor when the pressure heats up. Thank you for reminding me to lighten up. Taking situations—and myself—too seriously is one of my besetting faults."

"If that's all, you're doing well."

"I said *one* of my faults, but let's not go there." She grinned, green eyes sparkling.

Kent gaped, mesmerized. What was it with those eyes?

Lauren stepped toward him. "Since you've decided to be nice, I believe I will reward you."

Surely, she wasn't flirting with *him* now. Did he want her to do that? *Oh, yeah!* An ecstatic terror gripped him.

She pulled something from her pocket and held it out toward him. Slowly, he dropped his gaze toward her outstretched hand. Two strips of jerky? Air went out of his lungs like a punctured balloon.

She had brought him food. Did he want that? *Oh, yeah!* He grabbed the dried meat from her hand and ripped off a chunk with his teeth.

Lauren laughed. "Easy there, Wolfman. Should I have been worried about my fingers?"

"Not an unwise concern. My stomach was so flat it was starting to wrap around my backbone."

"While you eat, I'm going to talk to you about my *real* concerns."

"I can eat and listen at the same time." He tipped a strip of jerky in her direction.

"I'll hold you to that." She arched a brow. "At this point, I'm the only one in your confidence about the tandem parachute and the implications that item suggests about a saboteur among us. Everyone else is naturally assuming that if the plane was sabotaged the danger was left behind in civilization. All their attention is on our creepy mystery dweller, but no one is on their guard against each other. Now, I understand there are pros and cons about letting everyone in on our secret. If we speak up, the innocent will be informed about the danger, but the mutual paranoia will be a huge obstacle when we need to work together to survive. On the other hand, the guilty party will feel threatened, and that will either make him ultra-cautious and less dangerous or ultra-desperate and more dangerous."

"I vote for more dangerous," Kent said between bites. "The dude engineered a plane crash with himself on the plane. He's got guts—a high-stakes player—and he's not going to let anyone leave here alive but himself. He's already eliminated the main threat to exposure—his accomplice."

"You don't think our mystery dweller is behind the stovepipe issue and the other traps?"

"Let's say I'm not one hundred percent convinced."

"Surely, no one among us has a clue about how to set a Conibear trap."

"That's the only incident I think may have been a genuine accident. Makes sense that someone living up here by himself would set critter traps."

Lauren sighed heavily. "So where does that leave us?"

"I chose this burial spot so I could take a good look at my plane without making a big deal about it. If I find clear, physical evidence of sabotage to back up the circumstantial evidence of the parachute, I'm going to go all bad-cop on a bunch of Wall Street executives. Nobody else is going to die on my watch."

Please God, don't let that proclamation be empty bravado. Especially not when one of the dead could be this brave woman.

SEVEN

Lauren's stomach roiled as she hurried into the mercantile on Kent's heels. The guy looked like he was ready to tear someone's head off. Not that he'd really hurt anyone. Would he? Considering what he'd found when he examined the damage to his plane, she might not blame him if he threw a few punches. But they didn't have a clear idea who deserved the punches, and she really didn't need any more patients in her makeshift hospital.

The group was hunkered around the stove, talking—even Rich—but not Phil, who was hopefully snoozing with the aid of the painkiller Lauren had given him. All heads turned and chatter ceased as Kent loomed over them, holding up a misshapen lump of metal for their inspection.

"I want to know who this belongs to, and I want to know now."

Lauren studied reactions, as Kent would

likely be doing. Dirk scowled and looked away. Rich's brows drew together and he blinked. Cliff gaped at the object, expression blank. Neil pursed his lips and rubbed his whiskers. None of them said a word.

Her mom lifted a hand slowly as if she were in school. "Might I ask what that is?"

"It's a detonator." Kent's tone was thin ice. "Or what's left of it after the bomb it set off took out my electrical system and sent shrapnel into my fuel lines."

"It *was* sabotage," Cliff breathed out as if it were risky even to say the words.

Neil rose and planted his hands on his hips. "Why would you think one of us planted the bomb? That's nuts. We were all on the plane."

"Yeah," Dirk said. "One thing I'm not is a suicide bomber."

"Lauren." Kent glanced her way. "Would you grab that extra item from among my belongings...please?"

He spat the polite word as if it was a curse, but Lauren couldn't bring herself to take offense. The stakes were too high. They were gambling that a little pushback would goad the culprit into saying something incriminating or taking action that would expose him. Wound tight, she retrieved the large parachute pack and handed it to Kent.

He held it up beside the detonator. "This is a parachute. It was in the cargo bay that can be accessed from the lavatory. One of you was planning to evac and leave the rest of us to crash."

"But why?" Cliff burst out.

"Better question is how." Dirk stood up and dusted off his pants. "Any of the rest of you know how to parachute jump? I sure don't." He lifted his chin and crossed his arms in a "so there" posture.

"I do," Rich said. "Anyway, I jumped once about ten years ago. The whole experience was a rush, but I marked it off my bucket list and never did it again."

"Funny thing with this chute." Kent shook the pack. "None of you needs to know how to jump to use it."

Lauren's mom furrowed her brow. "That statement requires an explanation."

"I'm with Mrs. Barrington on that," Neil said.

"It's Nina. Everyone, please, just call me Nina."

"Very well, Nina," Kent said. "I'll explain myself, though one among you already knows the answer. This is a tandem chute. Two people jump in it—someone with skill and another person with little or no experience."

Dirk snorted. "Just who is this genius jumper that was going to hop out of the cargo bay attached to one of us?"

"There were two people aboard my aircraft with serious jump skills, me and my copilot. And since I chose to drive the plane, not jump out of it, that leaves one alternative."

"You mean..." Mom pressed a hand against her lips.

"Yeah, and happy day for her accomplice—or should I say the mastermind who either paid or blackmailed her into it—she's dead and can't talk."

"This is crazy!" Rich shook his head.

"I'm not buying it, either." Neil's wary gaze fixed on Kent.

"You might want to rethink that," Lauren said. "Kent's got logic on his side. The bomb had to be planted by someone with easy access to the plane *after* Kent signed off on the pre-flight maintenance. He explained that to me while we were examining the bomb damage. Then there's a tandem parachute in the cargo bay where the copilot did the loading. Sure thing one of us was planning to leave the plane with her. It's no stretch of the imagination to conclude that the same person among us conspired in the sabotage."

Silence fell for several heartbeats then Neil

spread his hands. "But, like Cliff asked, why did they do it?"

"When we know why, we'll know who." Lauren searched each face for a guilty tick, but they all looked like they'd been told the world was about to end.

"Who would want us all dead?" The whites showed around Rich's pupils. "We work for different companies. I didn't even know Neil or Cliff before today, though I've met Dirk and Phil a couple of times in the course of business. And I sure have never met Lauren or Mrs. B—Nina."

The group started babbling out competing thoughts and theories.

"Hold it!" Kent said, and silence fell. "There's another possibility. The target for extinction might have been only one of us, but the saboteur was willing to kill all to make sure the one died."

Mom lunged to her feet. "That's just despicable! Heinous!"

"This whole situation is heinous, Mom," Lauren said.

Her mother glared back at her. "When did you first know about the parachute? And don't tell me you just found out about it."

"I never lie, Mom."

"No, you just keep life-and-death information from your mother." Her blue eyes spat fire. "I need fresh air." She turned on her heel and headed for the back door with clipped steps.

Lauren followed, but Kent grabbed her sleeve. "I'll talk to her. I'm the one who told you to keep quiet."

She shook her head. "I'm the one who decided to go along with that. I need to talk to her."

Kent released her, and she quickly passed through the back storeroom and into the alley. Her mother leaned against the wall by the stairway, taking in deep breaths and letting them out slowly.

"I'm not sure I'm ready to have a conversation with you." Mom turned her head away.

An invisible fist punched Lauren's gut, but she stood her ground. "When have we had a chance to hold a conversation since our plane crashed, much less a private one?"

Mom sniffed and turned toward her. "That's no excuse. You could have made an opportunity."

"How about the opportunity you never made to tell me my father wasn't coming home?"

"That's different. You were a child."

"And you were the adult who knew the

truth, but didn't think your daughter could handle it so you pretended day after day that Daddy was coming back to us. We just had to wait and believe, you said. 'Maybe tomorrow,' you kept telling me. You let me hope for years about something that was never going to happen. I had to figure it out myself at the grand old age of eight and confront you before you admitted we'd been abandoned."

Tears filmed her mother's eyes. "I didn't know. I hoped he'd come back, too."

"It was a cruel hope."

"Only because it was based on what a fallible human being would do or not do." Her mother's hand gripped Lauren's forearm. "If I could change how I handled that horrible time, I would, but I never left you. God never left you."

"I know, Mom." A hard place inside her softened, and Lauren placed her hand atop her mother's. "You're a good mom, a good person. You didn't deserve to be hurt like that, either. I'm glad you finally got past it—better than me anyway—and found love again."

Her mother let out a watery chuckle. "Since you're all grown up now, I'll tell you a little secret. I had many opportunities to fall in love while you were a little girl, but I refused to take any of them because I couldn't take a chance on you getting hurt again."

"What do you mean?" Lauren's breathing hitched.

Mom's gaze locked on hers. "I've never been good at picking men. I seem to be attracted to all the wrong kinds—the bad boys. I know that about myself, and I didn't want you to pay the price ever again."

Lauren bit back an array of remarks about her mother's current smooth-talking husband. Her thoughts along that line were suddenly irrelevant. "So you waited until I was an adult to remarry? What a tremendous sacrifice. I'm stunned. I assumed you were as burned as I was and couldn't bring yourself to trust another man."

"Oh, honey, life's too short not to take a chance on love. Or as many chances as needed to get it right. So now that you know my secret, I want you to promise to give love a chance too."

Lauren laughed. "How did I know that any conversation with you was bound to return to my love life?"

"Or lack thereof."

"Guilty." She lifted her hands, palms out. "And guilty for not telling you about the parachute Kent found. I should have made the opportunity to give you a heads-up. I promise not to make that kind of mistake again."

Mom scowled. "That's not what I wanted you to prom—"

"I asked her to keep the information to herself until I checked out the plane," Kent said, stepping out into the alley.

Lauren narrowed her eyes at the too-attractive pilot. How much of her conversation with her mother had he overheard?

His gaze remained fixed on her mom, allowing her no opportunity to read his eyes. "I only told Lauren about the parachute yesterday so she would understand the urgency of speaking to Mags the instant she regained consciousness. But someone made sure that never happened."

Mom sucked in an audible breath. "I thought this mystery dweller that attacked Lauren caused all the smoke."

"Maybe. Maybe not. It seems suspicious to me that an incident was created designed to forever silence the most injured among us. Convenient for whoever had planned to exit the plane without the rest of us."

"Why didn't that happen?" Nina's brow puckered. "Wouldn't they have wanted to jump out before the bomb went off?"

"I think they were about to do it when the

bomb exploded prematurely, badly injuring Mags, and scuttling the escape plan."

"Makes sense." Lauren nodded.

Mom pursed her lips and cocked her head at Kent. "Am I a suspect?"

"Not much."

"Why not?"

"I can't see you ever hurting your daughter."

"Lots of parents do—in more ways than one." Mom slid a glance toward Lauren, but she pretended not to notice.

"It takes cold calculation to abandon your child to an airplane crash," Kent said. "You have the intelligence to plan it, Nina, but not the heart."

"Why, thank you, young man." Mom beamed up at him. "Have you decided on your chief suspect?"

"I'm still working on it."

"I'll let the two of you work on it together. You make a very good team." Mom patted Kent's arm. "I hear a broom calling me. Time to sweep out that front room so we don't have to keep sleeping in the dust." She disappeared into the mercantile, wearing a tiny smile.

Lauren frowned and tapped her foot. "She did it again."

"Yes, she did." Kent grinned.

Their gazes locked, and Lauren gaped at him as his grin faded and a special kind of warmth grew in his gray eyes. Her mouth went stone-dry, and her heart performed ridiculous acrobatics in her chest. Was he going to kiss her? Did she have the courage to let him?

Kent lowered his head toward Lauren's, giving her every chance to pull away. Alarm bells rang in his head, but he ignored them. This once, he'd live recklessly. His gut said the chance could be worth it. Their breaths mingled, lips brushed and—

"Lauren, come quickly!"

Neil's urgent tones from the doorway drew them apart. Lauren jumped backward, eyes wide as a fawn on a new day. Color washed up her face. Frustration balled Kent's fists, but he hid them at his sides as he positioned himself to hide Lauren's reaction from an onlooker and turned to face Neil.

"It's Phil," the older man said. "He's thrashing and calling for you, Lauren."

"I'll go to him." She rushed around Kent, brushed past Neil and disappeared into the building.

Neil stood aside as Kent followed.

"Sorry about that, man." Neil clapped him on the back with a knowing chuckle.

Kent took in a deep breath and let the comment slide. The guy hadn't done anything wrong, just bad timing. Or maybe good timing.

He could kick himself for letting emotions override his better judgment. Hadn't he learned anything about avoiding romance when a scheming parent was in the mix? Nina was kind of cute about her machinations, and she seemed to like him—something he couldn't say about the matriarch of Elspeth's family—but he wasn't about to risk involvement with a woman who was inclined to side with her parent over him in any decision they might try to make as a couple.

Then again, an almost kiss was no big deal. He'd had a moment of weakness. So what? He didn't have to let it happen again.

Then why was he suddenly more agitated by the loss of his kiss with Lauren than the loss of his plane?

Shaking his head at himself, he entered the mercantile and found Lauren crouched down in attendance on her groaning patient. She looked up at him as he stepped into her makeshift infirmary.

"I don't have any pain medication left other than over-the-counter pills. They aren't strong enough to do more than take the edge off. He

really needs an ice pack on that foot to re-
duce the swelling, but I used them on Rich
and Mags."

"The best we could do is a bucket of ice
water from the stream."

She gave a decisive nod. "We'll have to rig
up a chair so he can sit up to soak the foot and
alternate between that and lying down with
the foot elevated."

"I'll get on it with the others."

Kent sent Dirk, Neil and Cliff down to the
stream. Sending them out singly or in pairs
was out of the question now with any of
them under suspicion as a saboteur. Then he
took the wagon back out to the plane and removed a seat from the passenger cabin using
a small screwdriver in a mini-toolkit he carried around with him. They'd have to find a
way to screw the chair into the floor of the
mercantile without a drill, but somehow they'd
get the job done.

Upon his return to town, the other passengers were delighted to see the chair and
wanted to know when they could have one. He
promised that if they could get this chair fastened to the mercantile floor they could bring
the rest back with them, after properly bury-
ing Magdalena Haven. The planking proved
a challenge but with perseverance on Cliff's

part eventually the chair was sturdily in place without a drill. Teeth gritted, Phil was soon soaking his swollen, discolored foot in icy stream water.

Kent tasked the trio of Dirk, Cliff and Neil with chopping or scavenging more wood for the stove and seeing if they could find branches that could be turned into crutches for Rich, then he pulled Lauren aside. "I have to talk to Phil about the detonator and the parachute just like the others. If he's the guilty one, I need to see his reaction. If he's not, he deserves to know about the danger."

Up to that moment, she had studiously refused to meet his gaze. Probably as uncomfortable as he was about their near-kiss. But now she stared up at him, eyes dark and fierce. "I hate having my patient placed under more stress. Let's get this over with."

Kent retrieved the items and rejoined Lauren with her patient. He held the misshapen detonator toward Phil. "This was under the plane."

The man looked at the object, and his brows puckered. "You found a detonator? We were sabotaged! I knew it!"

"How do you know what a detonator looks like?"

Phil shrugged. "Straight out of high school,

I did a four-year tour with the army. Never saw combat though."

Kent showed him the parachute. "Do you know what this is?"

"I've seen one before. Never used one. Some kind of odd-looking parachute?"

"It's a tandem chute. Two people jump in it. This was in the cargo bay not labeled as anyone's property and not supposed to be there. The cargo bay can be accessed from the lavatory."

Kent fell silent, giving Phil an opportunity to put two and two together.

In a few seconds, the man's jaw fell open then he began shaking his head like a dog throwing off water. "Oh, no, you don't! You're not pinning that on me."

"You're a quick study."

Phil glared up at Kent. "You don't get far in arbitrage by being slow on the uptake."

"Fair enough, but now you know that we have to guard against each other, as well as whoever attacked Lauren."

Phil gave a grim nod. "If you want my opinion, keep an eye on Cliff. He's way too eager to help all the time—even in the office at Peerless One. The Boy Scout act is a little over the top."

"Noted."

Kent met Lauren's gaze. Her lips were pressed together in a thin line. He inclined his head toward the storage room. She offered a slight nod and headed in that direction. He motioned for Nina to join them, and she rose from her cushion by the stove.

In the dimness of the storage room, Lauren squared off in front of Kent. "That was just the first of many accusations between ourselves that we're going to be dealing with from now on."

"I know. It can't be helped."

Nina laid a hand on her daughter's arm. "It's frustrating, honey. I hate this, but it's not Kent's fault."

Lauren dropped her gaze. "Of course not. I just want answers. Like yesterday."

Looking from mother to daughter, Kent crossed his arms. "We're going to have to think this through. Who do either of you consider a top contender?"

Nina looked away and shifted her feet.

Lauren lifted her eyes to his. "It's got to be one of the Peerless One executives."

Nina flinched.

"Why do you think so?" Kent asked.

"They're the only ones who know each other well enough to have developed a reason to want one or more of the other ones dead."

"Spot-on. My conclusion exactly." His estimation of Lauren just rose another notch from its already high position.

Lauren's mother let out a little whimper.

Kent fixed her with a stern gaze. "What do you know that you're not telling us, Mrs. Barrington?" He purposely confronted her with the formal address.

"Not Marlin's company! I can't believe it...! Well, yes, I can believe it. I must!" She lifted her chin. "The FBI has been covertly sniffing around Peerless One. Even Marlin wasn't supposed to know about it, but he's got contacts. You know how it is in big business. You keep an ear to the ground." She shrugged. "He's been beside himself about it. To think that one or more of his executives might be doing something *illegal*!" She infused the last word with a wealth of repugnance. "If it were proven, the whole company and everyone connected to it would suffer, perhaps even be ruined."

Lauren frowned. "If the guilty executive or executives died in a plane crash, would that stop the investigation and save the company?"

"That's an awful thing to say!" Nina turned fierce eyes on her daughter. "*We* were on that plane!"

"I wasn't implying—"

"Yes, you were. I know you don't like Marlin. He can be overbearing at times, and he's got a ruthless reputation in business, but he's good to me, and that should mean something to you."

"It does, Mom. More than you know."

"Here's another possibility we need to consider," Kent interrupted. "Someone aboard that plane was planning to get off covertly before it went down. Probably to make it look like he must have died in the crash. Maybe one of the white-collar crooks wanted to kill his accomplices and disappear with the loot."

"That's a solid theory." Nina nodded.

Lauren scowled. "If you're right, Kent, we must be dealing with someone completely without conscience. He didn't care about the innocent lives on board."

Nina pursed her lips. "Or maybe he hates Marlin and wanted to hurt him by killing Lauren and me along with the others."

"You, anyway." Lauren's tone was wry. "I doubt anyone thinks I'm anything more than baggage that came along with the marriage."

"Daughter, I love you more than life itself, but sometimes I want to smack you. If you don't let go of that cynicism, you're going to wind up a lonely, friendless old lady one day." Nina stomped back into the front of the store.

"Ouch!" Kent rocked back on his heels.

Lauren's stare seemed focused on her toes. "On the rare occasion when my mom takes off the kid gloves, she knows how to land a knock-out punch. Unfortunately, she's more right than I'd like to admit. I just don't know how to fix myself."

"None of us can do that. Not on our own, anyway."

She jerked her head up, nostrils flaring. "Don't you think I've asked God a million times?"

"Probably. But do you keep Him at arm's length, too?"

Without another word or glance, she imitated her mother's rigid-backed stomp away from him. Kent let out a heavy sigh. Another home run with Lauren Carter.

He set about organizing the transportation of his copilot's body to her hopefully temporary resting place. He insisted that every able-bodied person accompany the hearse to the burial site, except for Lauren, who stayed with her patients. Neither one was able to be a threat to anyone at the moment, though either of them could have been in on the sabotage of the plane, and Phil, at least, could have been the one who stopped up the mercantile stove and set the booby trap at the blacksmith shop.

After their sad chore, the group returned to

the mercantile with all of the seats from the plane. The couch didn't need to be screwed into the floor in order to be stable for seating. Nina settled on that piece of furniture, gaze faraway and pensive. Cliff and Dirk worked at fastening the chairs around the perimeter of the stove.

Kent took Neil and headed to the stream for another bucket of water. They all needed hydration again soon. The older man went without complaint, but flagging steps and dark smudges highlighted the slight bags under his eyes, betraying bone-deep weariness.

When they were out of earshot of the others, he glanced up at Kent. "Since you didn't take off alone with your trusty sidearm but requested my humble presence, I assume you need to talk to this old mossback privately."

Kent chuckled. "No moss growing on your intellect. I'll get around to picking everyone's brain eventually. So, what's your theory? How did we end up here and by whose hands?"

Neil offered a toothy grin. "I appreciate your directness, though you stopped short of asking me if I'm the culprit. A confession would certainly help the course of justice along, though if we can't get back to so-called civilization, it wouldn't be worth much. Unless, of course, we form a lynch mob."

Kent shot a sharp stare at his companion. "That was morbid."

"It was, but it's the way everyone feels. We can hardly look at each other anymore. That scene around the grave site—everyone staring at the mound of dirt, wondering who is going to be next and whose neck they can wring for it, and you offering a prayer and kind words for the dear departed. Hypocritical of you, by the way."

Kent's jaw tightened. "I didn't think so. I don't excuse what she did—can't even comprehend it—but she'll be judged by the highest court in the universe, and that's not me."

Neil stopped walking, and Kent halted a few feet away. The older man searched his face for long, quiet moments.

"You really believe that," he said at last.

"I do." Kent started walking again. Evening was coming on, and with it, a bitter chill that dug through his bomber jacket. "Don't you?"

Neil fell into step. "Sometimes I wish I did, but most of the time I'm glad I don't. It's not a judgment I care to face. I'm no saint, and that is as much of a confession of my life story as will have to suffice."

"I'd feel the same way if I hadn't already engaged the only lawyer guaranteed to prevail in that courtroom."

"Let's not even go there." He waved a dismissive hand. "You want to know what my theory is about our plane crash. The only suspects that make sense are the guys from Peerless One. Rumors are starting to get around in arbitrage circles that something's not right."

"Do you know any specifics?"

"No."

"Any names?"

"No."

"If you think of anything, will you tell me?"

"You got it."

They finished their errand and returned to the mercantile to find everyone clustered around the stove, as usual, only now they had seats off the floor. Even Phil was sitting up, pained expression on his pudgy face and bandaged foot propped on an extra seat. Rich was getting along without keeping his leg elevated, though discomfort showed in the tension around his mouth. In typical fashion, Cliff was making himself useful attempting to rig up crutches with notched sticks they'd chopped down and T-shirts he was trying to tie just right to create a cushion for Rich's armpits. Looked like a tedious project.

Dirk greeted them with a grumble about drinking water out of the same bucket where Phil soaked his foot, but Nina shushed him with a reminder that they boiled the water before drinking it, and there was plenty of tea and instant coffee from the airplane galley. A meal of jerky and canned peaches from the mystery dweller's hut was consumed in sullen silence.

"How are everyone's cell phones holding out?" Kent asked as they finished eating.

"What does that matter?" Dirk snorted. "There's no service."

"Not down here in the bottom of the valley, but I got to thinking today. We haven't tried climbing one of the cliffs to see if service is available higher up. The clouds will break eventually, maybe even by morning. We need to do two things tomorrow—place glass shards on the roof, and then we need to climb a section of cliff-side and plant as many of those glass pieces as we can as high up as we can reach. No guarantees, but we might as well check for service while we're at it."

Faces brightened, and the able-bodied scattered to retrieve their phones.

"My cell's about to give up," Cliff called, "but I've got one of those external batteries. I'll charge it right up."

It turned out that most of the passengers had wireless chargers, including Lauren. Nina, Rich and Neil were exceptions, but Neil claimed he'd been keeping his cell turned off and had half a charge left. Nina had forgotten to turn hers off and had little juice left, but she shut hers down to conserve what was there. Rich's phone was already toast, and he apologized for not having his head in the game.

"Understandable." Nina patted him on the arm. "You won't be climbing any cliffs tomorrow anyway."

"Me either," Dirk announced. "I've got a phobia about heights." He crossed his arms and stuck out his chin, challenging anyone to argue with him.

Kent sent him a pleasant smile. "Then you, Nina and Neil can go scavenging for more wood for the stove, haul in more water, bring more food and supplies from the mystery dweller's cabin, and then gather as many pine cones as you can find from under the trees. Don't pick any off the branches. Those will be too green to yield edible pine nuts."

Grumbling under his breath something about crazy nuts and slave drivers, Dirk withdrew from the group and began laying out his blankets for bedtime.

"And by the way," Kent called to him, "you and Cliff are taking first watch."

"What watch?"

Cliff let out a huff. "In case you missed the

memo, DJ, someone out there and/or in here is trying to kill us. We have to do whatever we can to make sure they don't succeed, including missing a little shut-eye."

"But why two of us, Mr. Brown Nose? Just because you've turned into our fearless leader's mindless slave doesn't mean I have to do the same."

Lauren leaped to her feet. "Can it, you two. Bickering and name-calling isn't helping anyone. Can't you see that two guards can keep an eye on each other as well as watch for any threats from the outside? And until any of you have better ideas how we can survive in the middle of nowhere, get your attitudes right."

"Hear, hear." Nina toasted with her cup of tea.

Kent rose slowly. "Okay, now that we've gotten that out of our systems, Lauren is correct that the pairing up has a purpose. Multiple purposes, actually. First, since the threat could be from within and from without, the guards can help keep each other safe, come running at any cry of alarm. Second, the opposite is true. The guards need to guard each other. One of you will be assigned to the back door, the other to the front, but you will switch stations every half hour. If one of you has disappeared from his station, possibly to wreak some of the mayhem we've already experienced, wake me up immediately. Any questions?" No one answered. "Good. You'll be replaced every four hours. The next shift belongs to Neil and—"

"—Me." Rich finished Kent's sentence. "I may not have two good legs at the moment, but I've got two good ears and eyes. No one will get by me, in or out, or they'll taste my trusty staff." He swung the improvised crutch like a bat.

"Hey, watch out with that thing!" Cliff ducked, laughing.

Everyone chuckled. The laughter felt good. Therapeutic. Kent took a deep breath, and thanked God for this moment.

Less than four hours later, he was jerked out of the best sleep he'd had in the past forty-eight hours. Dirk was screaming like an opera soprano and shaking him.

Kent heaved into a sitting position, hand curling automatically around the pistol under his head cushion. With his other hand, he grabbed the hysterical man's bony shoulder. "What's happened?"

"It's Cliff!" The man was panting like he'd just run a mile. "He's dead. He's just…dead!"

EIGHT

Not fully awake, Lauren lunged to her feet. As the meaning of Dirk's shrieking sunk in, her heart pounded like a mariachi dancer.

"Where is he?" She lit the kerosene lamp on a nearby shelf.

"By the b-back door." Dirk's words faltered.

The rest of the party roused with murmurs of alarm as Lauren grabbed the first-aid kit and headed for the storage room.

Kent darted in front of her, gun in his right hand. "I'll go first."

She followed at his heels, lamp held high to illuminate the space. No one lurked in the storage room, except for Cliff, who sat slumped against the wall by the back door. Lauren rushed to him, knelt and set the lamp down. A mug lay tipped over by Cliff's side, and a small splotch of dark liquid stained the floorboards.

She checked the pulse at his neck and his

wrist then looked up at Kent, who hovered grim-faced. "He's alive. Barely. If I had to guess, I'd say someone drugged his coffee, but in order to treat, I need to know what type of drug we're dealing with." She pulled the small flashlight from her kit and examined first one eye then the other. "Pinpoint pupils, depressed respiration. Most likely a narcotic."

"What can we do for him?"

Lauren scrambled in her kit. "Here it is. Thank You, Lord! I thought I saw this."

"What is it?"

"Naloxone auto-injector. If he's not too far gone, this stands a good chance of counteracting the overdose." She administered the injection as the rest of the party crowded around.

"Back, everyone!" Kent barked. "Give them space."

She rummaged in the kit. "No activated charcoal. If we could have forced that down him, it would have absorbed any narcotic remaining in his stomach." She looked up at Kent. "Help me get him laid out in the infirmary. I need to intubate to aid his breathing."

Cliff was not a small man, and Lauren expected several helpers would be needed in the transport, but Kent slung Cliff over his shoulder and hustled to the infirmary without a hitch in his stride. Lauren scrambled to follow. She shouldn't have been surprised. Soldiers were trained in evacuating the injured.

Mom's firmest tones admonished the others to stay on their own side of the partition. In this moment, Lauren didn't mind that her mother could be a miniature major general.

She finished the intubation and sat back on her haunches to wait. Long seconds ticked past in a silence that crimped Lauren's lungs like the very room was holding its breath. A soft groan left the patient, and his chest began to rise and fall visibly, where before his breathing had been undetectable. Tears stung the backs of Lauren's eyes and one crept onto her eyelash.

Blinking rapidly, she gazed up at Kent. "He was deep in the woods, but he's on the way back."

A smile flickered on Kent's lips, and he squeezed her shoulder. "He can thank God you were here with us."

Lauren dropped her gaze. How many more passengers might need her services before this ordeal was over? What if she couldn't save them all? She'd already lost one. The supplies in the first-aid kit weren't intended to last for long, and they were already dwindling dramatically.

"Since no narcotics are in the first-aid kit,"

Kent said, "the drugs used to lace the coffee were not stolen from the kit."

Lauren's breath hitched. "That means someone has their own supply."

"What would we be looking for specifically?"

"The list is fairly long for the treatment of anxiety or chronic pain like Xanax, Diazepam, Oxycontin or Hydrocodone, to name a few. You're going to search luggage?"

Lips thinning, Kent jerked a nod.

"Don't be too surprised if you uncover a treasure trove of such prescriptions," she said. "The lifestyle these guys live makes it almost certain they'll be treated with opioids or sedatives at some point in their distinguished careers."

Something like a growl left Kent's throat. Lauren totally got the frustration. She was vexed too—and not only about the physical jeopardy they were all in.

What about that kiss she and Kent had almost shared? The guy was more of a danger to her heart than she would have thought possible. Must be the stressful situation. Surely, if—no, when—they got out of this valley and back to civilization, she'd look back on this intense attraction as a fleeting madness.

Why did that sensible idea feel like a stone in her heart?

"We have to take a look in the luggage anyway," Kent said. "Maybe we can expose someone with fewer pills in their bottle than ought to be there."

He walked away, and Lauren took in a deep, quivering breath. *Lord, help us stop this monster before someone else dies at his hands.* The straightforward prayer left her heart with a fervency that she'd lacked since...well, ever.

"Everyone get your luggage out of the storage room and bring it in here." Kent's deep tones hacked into the murmur of strained voices outside the infirmary. "We are conducting a search for narcotics, and from this point on, our belongings will be kept out in the open under the eyes of us all."

"Wait just a minute, you can't just go rummaging—"

"I will toss your things from one end of this room to the other if I must." Kent interrupted Dirk's petty outrage. "Far better if you form an orderly queue and submit to a voluntary search. If you have nothing to hide, that is."

"I may as well tell you that I take Xanax," Neil said.

Anti-anxiety medication—Lauren mentally cataloged the drug.

"If you must know, I take Klonopin," Dirk volunteered in a grudging growl.

Given Dirk's tendency to avoid any stressful activity, Lauren surmised the prescription was for panic attacks. Why did he stay with the profession he was in? Money? Powerful motivator.

"Oh, just great!" Rich's exclamation emerged like a mournful sigh. "I may as well confess."

Heart twisting, Lauren rose from her patient's side and stepped around the shelving to the common area. "What have you done?"

The executive dropped his gaze. "I have prescription Oncet for a bad back. I've been hoarding it for myself since my knee got injured. I should have been sharing it with Phil." He pulled a pill bottle from his pants pocket.

"You didn't lace Cliff's coffee with it?"

Rich's mouth dropped open then shut with a clack of teeth. "No! Why would I want to hurt Cliff? He's been such an asset to us all in this mess."

"That's exactly why someone wanted to hurt him," Kent said. "Now, please go get your luggage, everyone. What I said stands. We're going to search and see what conclusions we can draw. Lauren, please take possession of Rich's prescription bottle and count the contents. If the date of fill and number of pills remaining don't match, let me know. I believe we will entrust all our prescriptions to your care from now on. You can dispense them as we need them."

With haunted expressions and soft mutters, the passengers complied. Lauren returned to her patients. Cliff's eyelids were fluttering, and he moaned a little. She could possibly remove the airway as soon as he came fully awake. Phil lay unmoving in his spot with his eyes closed, face pale and foot elevated, but the agitation in his breathing betrayed that he was awake.

Lauren knelt beside him. "Rich has offered to share his prescription painkiller with you. Would you like that?"

The man nodded, and she administered the medication. Then she counted the pills remaining and compared that figure to what should be there. The number matched. Rich had not used these pills to overdose Cliff.

The harsh hiss of zippers and snapping of locks from the other side of the partition indicated the luggage search was under way. Lauren rose and took up a post near the end of the shelving unit that separated her infirmary from the common area. From there, she could monitor her patients and observe the progress of the luggage search at the same time. Particularly, she focused on the body language of Dirk and Neil, the remaining able-bodied executives. Dirk paced, scowling. Neil stood still, rubbing his bristly chin. Typical behaviors for them.

While Kent riffled through the luggage contents, Lauren's mother stood by with a pad and paper and took notes. Then she received any confiscated medication containers into an airplane emesis bag. Quite a number of snack foods were also unearthed and set aside for sharing at meal times.

"I have a question." Lauren interrupted the proceedings.

Kent's stormy gaze fixed on her. "Go ahead."

"Did Cliff make his own coffee, or did someone make it for him?"

Her mother let out a soft groan and turned toward Lauren. "It was me. I made it for him." All eyes fixed on her. "I made a cup for Dirk, too."

Kent stepped in front of Dirk, halting his pacing. "Where is your coffee cup?"

Blinking rapidly, the smaller man pointed toward the front door. "O-over there. Where I was stationed."

"Bring it to me."

Steps choppy, gaze lowered, Dirk complied.

Kent frowned into the mug. "This is nearly full. You didn't drink it. Why?"

"Well…you see…I—uh…"

"You knew it was poisoned!" Neil burst out. "Probably because you put the narcotic in there yourself."

Dirk's face flamed. "That's crazy, you useless old coot! I'm not stupid. If I wanted to make sure to look innocent, I would have put only a little narcotic in my coffee and downed it."

"You're displaying your devious mind, Dirk." Lauren stepped forward and took the mug from Kent. She swirled the contents and sniffed. Then she dipped a fingertip into the brew and placed a drop on her tongue. Acrid, but no more so than strong instant coffee usually was. "I can't tell if this is laced with anything. The coffee taste and smell is too strong."

"Doesn't matter," Kent said. "I know why Dirk didn't drink it."

"Do tell." Dirk crossed his arms over his chest and lifted his chin.

"You fell asleep, probably right away. In fact, I doubt you attempted to change places with Cliff even once during your shift. And while you snoozed, Cliff drank his coffee and nearly died."

"I couldn't help it." Dirk turned his back on everyone. "I was exhausted."

"Never mind." Kent held up a translucent, brown medicine container. No pills were inside. "I found this in Magdalena Haven's luggage."

Lauren took the vial and read the label. "Vicodin. Why was she on such a strong pain reliever?" She gazed up at Kent.

He grimaced. "About a year ago she was involved in a car accident. Cracked a couple of vertebrae. When she came to work with me six months ago, she checked out perfect with her physical exam and signed off that she no longer took prescription pain relievers that might slow her reaction time, which was, apparently, a lie."

"Addicted, I'm guessing," Lauren said. "Someone among us knew they would find these in her luggage, implying intimate acquaintance with Ms. Haven."

Neil slapped his arms against his sides. "How are we supposed to prove that any among us knew your copilot, Garland? Vetting her qualifications was on you!"

Color leached from Kent's face. "I agree. I trusted when I shouldn't have done."

Lauren shook her head. "Were your pre-employment procedures for Mags any different for her than for anyone else?"

"No."

"Then I don't see fault here. Unfortunately, I have learned by bitter experience that those who should be the closest to us can turn out to be the least worthy of our trust."

Lauren averted her gaze from her mother's much-tried expression. Mom made no secret that she thought Lauren should be over her father's desertion by now. Was that something a person *could* get over? Clearly, Mom's sunny disposition had helped her move on. Didn't she see that Lauren would love to do the same, but had never found the way? She was like a lab mouse forever stuck in the maze without ever reaching the reward.

The rest of the night passed in fitful dozing. Lauren rose shortly after dawn, grumpy and gritty-eyed. None of the others looked any better than she felt. Breakfast was—surprise!—jerky. Cliff woke up as she washed the last of her dried meat down with lukewarm water. He tried to talk, but the airway prevented him. Lauren removed it, and he let out a long sigh and sat up.

"What happened?" His voice was a hoarse croak.

"Someone laced your coffee with narcotics. We nearly lost you."

The man's jaw dropped. "No wonder I

feel like I've been dragged through a knothole backward."

A shadow stole over them, and Lauren looked up to find Kent standing there. He handed Cliff a container of water. The man eagerly downed it.

Kent squatted by their side. "Did anyone approach you after you took up your post with your coffee?"

Cliff's brow knotted. Finally, he shook his head. "I don't think so, but my memories of last evening are fuzzy. I barely remember being told I was to stand first watch with Dirk. Nothing after that."

Lauren's gaze met Kent's. No help there in narrowing the field of suspects.

Kent rose and left the infirmary area. "Listen up, people! I know we're all dog-tired and cranky, but we have some important assignments today." Attentive silence fell. "The clouds are breaking up, and the sun is making guest appearances. Our first order of business is to place glass shards on the roof and as high up the sides of the cliffs as we can get and to check for cell service up there. Considering the threat level among us, we ablebodied are going to stick together for this task. No exceptions."

"I'm on it," Cliff said, attempting to rise.

Lauren pressed him back down.

Kent shook his head. "There's no way you can climb rocks when you're still wobbly and woozy. Stay here with Phil and Rich. Maybe you'll be better this afternoon, and we can all go out foraging."

Cliff's lips thinned but he nodded.

Lauren looked from Kent to her patients and back again. "I want to help lay out the glass and search for cell phone signals, but maybe I should stay with the people who are hurt."

Rich laughed and waved a hand. "None of us is in a life-threatening condition. We're not likely to need medical care in the next couple of hours. Go on with the rest."

Cliff and Phil nodded affirmation. Still torn, Lauren murmured a soft assent.

"I'll stay with the injured," Dirk piped up. "Like I told you, I can't handle heights."

Kent jabbed a finger at him. "You are coming with us. If nothing else, you can sit at the base of the cliff and call out if you see anything suspicious."

Grumbling and sullen, Dirk followed on Lauren's heels out the door.

When the group reached the plane, everyone wrapped a good-sized shard of windshield glass in a piece of clothing from their luggage. The signal on the mercantile roof was soon laid, and then they returned to the plane for more glass.

"We're going to follow the stream toward the cliff face," Kent announced. "It behooves us to check out how the water leaves the valley. Probably it goes underground, but on the off chance it offers an escape, we need to know."

Faces brightened at the thought, and the onward trek was accompanied by the mutter of swift water across rocks. Breaks in the cloud cover were more frequent than yesterday, and the temperature had become milder. Still, Lauren shivered beneath her layers of clothing. Her chill perhaps had little to do with the outward atmosphere. A ruthless and cunning killer walked among them. Who was it?

Lauren studied the others. Dirk trudged along, head down and scowling. Neil held his head high, but his jaw muscles flexed as if he were grinding his teeth. Kent led them, his broad back straight and confident, stride long and easy. Mom scurried beside Lauren closely enough that they shared warmth.

"It's got to be Dirk," her mother murmured.

"Why do you say that?"

"I don't like him, and I do like Neil."

Lauren stifled a wry chuckle. "Agreed,

but lots of likable people commit crimes and plenty of jerks are technically honest."

"A hateful truth. I suppose Rich could have put the drug in Cliff's coffee. He gets around well enough with those crutches now. But he couldn't have stopped up the stovepipe or arranged that potentially deadly accident at the blacksmith shop."

Lauren shuddered at the memory of rusty rake teeth stabbing toward her vulnerable flesh. "Our mystery dweller could have done those things. For sure, he set the Conibear trap, though not necessarily intending to catch a human. We city folk would have no idea how to set traps."

"Which leaves us exactly where?"

"Confused."

They halted at the base of the cliff, where the stream abruptly disappeared into a cleft in the rocks. A collective groan went up. No way could a person wedge himself into the gap, unless he went underwater, hoping that the opening widened into a navigable cave. And then who knew where that cave might lead? Nobody was ready to take the plunge.

"Well, that's that." Kent turned to face them. "Onward and upward. Spread out so that there is a regular distance between us of a couple dozen yards. Maintain the separation as you climb as far as you feel you can safely go. Then find a flat, stable surface where you can leave your piece of glass. If a search plane spots these reflections at regular intervals, they will know the formation is not natural and come investigate."

"When should we try our cell phones?" Dirk held his up.

Everyone went silent, staring at him.

"Wha-a-at?" he said.

"I thought you were scared of heights and weren't going to climb." Neil's tone held a sneer.

Dirk went bright red. "I want to get rescued more than any of you. Since you dragged me out here, I'm going to climb as high as I can make myself."

"All right. Good for you," Kent said in a moderate tone. "To answer Dirk's valid question, try your cell phones as frequently as you want, but especially when you reach your highest possible elevation. In fact, send a text message to everyone on your contact lists, naming our location as Trouble Creek, Nevada. Sometimes a text will get through even when it appears there is no cell service. Any other questions?" No one spoke. "Let's get to it."

Ten minutes later, sweat trickled down the

back of Lauren's neck as she climbed. She'd come past the initial easy slope and now picked her way among jumbled rock formations that occasionally offered steps up and sometimes presented barriers to be climbed over. From somewhere on her right hand, her mother's progress could be heard but not seen. Glancing above and to the left, Kent's large figure made progress. He was a moving landmark—an inspiration to keep on going.

Lauren paused and checked her cell. No service bars. She sent a text nonetheless then continued upward. At last, she pulled herself onto a wide ledge and stopped to rest. The noises from her mother's side had ceased. Perhaps Mom had reached her maximum height, left her glass shard and was on the way down. Lauren could only hope. A sudden *chink, chink, chink* of falling stone far to her left let her know that Kent still climbed.

Seated on the lip of the ledge, she gazed into the valley below. The sun had come out full force about the time they discovered that the stream disappeared underground, and the wreckage of the plane gleamed dully—itself a possible rescue beacon. The town of Trouble Creek was a sparse collection of mud-brown buildings.

Wait a minute. Was someone moving

around along the edge of the town? At this distance, all she could make out was a speck, but it was definitely traveling. Either she was seeing a large animal or a human being. Could it be Cliff? He was the most mobile among those they'd left behind. If so, why had he left the mercantile? Maybe it was the mystery dweller. Were those they'd left down below in danger?

Sucking in a breath, Lauren stood and strained her eyes toward the movement skirting the abandoned mining village. A rustle of sound caught her ear. Not from below. From behind her! The breath froze in her lungs. She commanded herself to turn, but it was as if her body had become like the very rocks she stood upon.

A low, feral growl grew in intensity. Every hair on Lauren's body stood to attention as she whirled, hands raised in defensive posture. A towering mass of fur lumbered toward her on its hind legs. A bear. Yet not a bear. She caught only a glimpse of the horrific creature as she screamed, stumbled backward and plunged off the ledge.

Lauren's scream shot through Kent like a geyser of ice water. Praying frantically, he made his way down. If anything had happened to that glorious woman, he'd—what? He stuffed the panic down. Couldn't think like that right now. Getting to her as quickly as possible was the only focus.

At last he reached a decent-sized ledge. The scream had come from somewhere near here. His gaze was snagged by a small, unnatural movement. Something was caught, waving in the breeze, between a pair of small boulders near the lip of the ledge. He went closer and leaned down. Fur! He plucked the tuft of hairs from the chink in the rocks and stuffed it into his jacket pocket.

A human groan sent his heart into overdrive. Peering over the ledge, he found Lauren's crumpled figure about eight feet below, draped over a very small ledge that interrupted a sheer drop of lethal distance. The drop-off ended in a set of rocks jutting up like serrated teeth. If Lauren stirred more than a few inches, she'd tumble over, and those teeth would chew her up.

"Lauren," he called with soft urgency. "Lauren, stay still."

Another groan answered him. She lifted her head and peered up at him, gaze disoriented.

"Make only very small movements," he told her. "You're on the edge of a drop-off."

She blinked, and her face paled as comprehension entered her eyes.

"Are you hurt?"

She shook her head. "I don't think so. Bruised, maybe."

Kent exhaled a long breath. *Thank You, God!* If she'd broken a bone, who knew how he would get her to safety.

"Okay. I need you to stand up very carefully. If you stand and reach for me, I should be able to pull you up here."

Kent stretched out flat on his stomach and extended his arms toward her as she eased to her feet, clinging closely to the cliff face.

Crack!

A chunk of her narrow ledge broke way, staggering her. With a shriek, she flung her arms upward, and Kent caught her wrists.

"Don't stop!" he called. "Scramble up here."

He pulled for all he was worth, and she practically lunged up the wall into his arms. They clung together on their knees, shaking and breathing hard.

"You're okay now. You're all right." He kept repeating those words as her soft sobs sent tremors through him.

At last, she lifted her head. Those jade-colored eyes shimmered with tears. He wanted to hold her and never stop. Keep her safe forever.

The rattle of falling rock stabbed ice into his core. Kent broke away from Lauren and whirled, hand on his sidearm.

Nina stood a few feet away, but her gaze was not on them. Her eyes were wide and fixed on the valley. Slowly, she lifted her arm and pointed.

"Fire!"

NINE

All but Phil and Rich stood staring at the burned-out hulk of the small cabin where the mystery dweller had kept vital supplies. Everything they hadn't yet moved to the mercantile was toast now. Long columns of smoke drifted upward, tainting the air with acrid odor.

Lauren's gut churned. Her hands made tight fists. If only she had someone's face to bury them in she might actually let swing. Whoever did this had it coming.

"At least none of the other buildings caught fire," Cliff muttered.

"The whole town could have gone up in flames," Neil said. "Then where would we stay to keep warm?"

Lauren glanced over at Kent, who stood with his hands in his pockets, face set like granite. For a few moments on that ledge while he'd held her, she'd allowed herself to feel safe, protected. An illusion, of course. Here was reality.

"This was no accident," she said. "When I was up on the cliffs, I saw someone sneaking around the edge of the town like he was up to no good. I couldn't make out who it was, but with Kent, Neil, Dirk, my mom and me rock-climbing, that doesn't leave many options."

All eyes narrowed on Cliff.

"It wasn't me. Phil and Rich can vouch I stayed indoors right up until we smelled the smoke, and I came running. But there was nothing I could do except watch this place burn." He spread his hands. "Then you guys showed up all out of breath."

"The mystery dweller strikes again," Lauren's mom pronounced in clipped syllables.

"Why would he burn his own place down?" Dirk asked.

"To keep us from getting his stuff," Neil said.

"Seems pretty drastic." Dirk hugged himself.

"Our whole situation is pretty drastic, DJ." Cliff's tone was more tired than snide.

"Let's get back to the mercantile, everyone," Kent directed. "We need to haul in more water and then start seriously foraging for provisions. No one, I repeat, no one goes out alone."

At midafternoon, while the others were hunkered around the stove extracting nuts from pine cones, Lauren volunteered to accompany Kent on a fishing expedition to the creek—a literal fishing expedition. He had managed to fashion a pole from a stout stick, thick thread from the telltale parachute and a hook from a safety pin contained in her mom's travel sewing kit. They would either find bait by digging for worms at the creek's edge or default to bits of jerky.

"What do you know?" Kent chuckled as they left the warmth of the mercantile. "Your mother hardly seemed to notice we left together."

Lauren smiled, but humor quickly faded. "Just goes to show how worried she is about other things."

"I don't blame her. And, as much as I wish your sole motivation in volunteering for this excursion was to be with me, I suspect you have an ulterior motive. Is there something you need to tell me?"

They stopped and faced each other along the path that was beginning to be worn by the party's many trips to the creek. Heart beating raggedly, Lauren searched Kent's face. Did he mean what he said about wanting her to want to be with him? Probably just that life and death moments tended to bring out intensity of feelings that wouldn't otherwise be there. Besides, this was an impossible time to consider romance. She ran her tongue across her teeth and looked away.

"Yes, something I need to talk to you about." She started onward toward the creek, and he fell into step without further comment. She took his silence as an invitation to continue her story. "When I was up on that ledge—before I fell—something...no, someone came at me."

"Something? Someone? Which is it?"

"I wish I knew." She shuddered. "It was huge—taller than you. It stood on its hind legs and was covered in fur."

"A bear?"

"That's just it. The face was not a bear's. It was human. Sort of."

"Can you be more specific?"

Lauren stopped again and squared off with Kent. "You don't believe me."

"On the contrary, I believe you totally." He dug in his jacket pocket and produced a tuft of fur. "I found this up there."

Lauren closed her eyes and swallowed. Hard.

She looked up at Kent. "What was it? I was terrified. That's why I tumbled off the ledge."

"Could be our mystery dweller. Makes sense that he'd swaddle himself in furs to keep warm."

"But if the mystery dweller was up on the cliffs with me, who was sneaking around starting fires in Trouble Creek?"

"Maybe we've got more than one mystery dweller...or maybe the saboteur among us is cleverer than we ever imagined."

"What does that mean?"

"Means I'm going to be doing some serious thinking while I'm fishing."

"Ditto."

"Good. Let's bounce ideas off each other. We might even come up with a plan."

Lauren's insides warmed. This man treated her like part of his team, actually acted like he needed and appreciated her. She'd never allowed herself to be treated like arm candy by any of the guys she'd sporadically dated, but none of them had made her feel like her thoughts and opinions might impact their choices. Could that possibly be because she'd always picked men whose careers meant more to them than any person? Had that choice on her part been calculated to keep the relationships superficial? The better to guard her heart?

She snorted through her nose and shook herself. Where had these navel-gazing thoughts come from?

Kent shot her a narrow look. "Not coming down with a cold, are you?"

"Not a bit," she responded lightly and quickened her pace.

No way could she allow him to gaze too deeply into her jade eyes, as he dubbed them. He might see the rapidly growing cracks in her armor. She wasn't ready to be that vulnerable yet.

"Why do you call me Jade Eyes?" *Yikes!* Clearly, her mouth filter was not working.

"Not many people have your vivid shade of green. It's extraordinary. Besides, I didn't know your name when I started calling you that. Does it bother you?"

She opened her mouth, shut it and shrugged. "Of course not." The glib answer following a significant pause didn't sound convincing, even to herself.

"Hmmm. Your no-no sounds more like a yes-yes. You don't have to explain yourself. I'll cut it out."

Lauren stuffed her hands into her jacket pockets. A moment ago they'd been cold, but now she just wanted to wipe the sweat off her palms on the pocket linings. So much for not being vulnerable. What did she tell him? Sure, he said she didn't have to explain, but dropping the subject just felt...cowardly. And dishonest. To him and to herself.

They reached the creek bank where the beavers had created their pond, and Kent handed her the makeshift pole while he began to dig in the soft, moist dirt.

"It's so chilly," he said, "I don't know if we'll find earthworms. Maybe we can turn over a few rocks and uncover a grub or two, though the cold will make those less plentiful also. Then again, if we find enough, we could fry them up and eat them instead of fish."

"Ewww! You're just torturing me for not satisfying your curiosity about your nickname for me."

"Not at all. I was—and am—completely serious. They taste like—"

"Chicken, right?"

"More like crunchy nothing with a mildly nutty aftertaste."

"You've actually eaten them?"

"Locusts and honey too. Quite biblical. Aha!" He bent down and came up with a sluggishly wriggling night crawler. "Pull up a rock, and let's do some fishing."

They settled down on matching boulders near the still pond. Kent flicked his line out into the deeper middle of the water. They sat and waited. And waited.

He sighed. "It may be that the water has grown too cold up here, and the fish have migrated downstream. I figured if any were left alive, they would be trapped in the pond."

"Let's not give up yet." Lauren laid her right hand over his left, which rested on his thigh.

He curled his fingers around hers, and she didn't pull away. Not just because she enjoyed the warmth on her chilled digits. The touch soothed a troubled place inside her. Never had closeness with another human being generated peace rather than wariness. Even with her mother, she had to be on her guard around certain topics.

How weird and how very nice.

"Okay. I'll tell you."

Kent didn't look her way. Didn't respond except to flick his line back and forth.

"When I was little, my father called me Jadie-girl, sometimes Jadie-Sadie, and every once in a while, Jade Eyes."

"The memory hurts you? Did he pass away?"

"Hardly." Her upper lip curled. "He mostly lived with us when I was very small."

"Mostly?"

"Let's just say, he'd come home and stay for a few months then he'd be gone a few months. Mom always told me he was away on business, and I bought the whitewash when I was little. Then on my fifth birthday—poof!—he left and never came back. Mom tried to keep up the charade about the business trip. I even tried to believe her for a few more years, but I couldn't forget that I overheard the last thing he said to my mom. 'Nina-baby, I didn't sign up for this. You know I can't live with a couple of cement blocks wrapped around my feet, weighing me down. You and Jadie-girl—well, I've got to be free.' End quote."

"What a selfish jerk…! No offense."

"None taken. Now that I'm grown up, my sentiments exactly. When I was a kid, all I understood was that I'd been rejected. I didn't measure up. I wasn't worth sticking around for, and I was a burden to the one man who should have been first in line to love me unconditionally."

"Wow." Soft silence fell, and then Kent cleared his throat. "May I make an observation without taking my life in my hands?"

"No guarantees." She added a soft laugh, but her pulse pounded in her throat.

Why did this moment feel so awful and so

awesome at the same time? A risk-taker in relationships she was not, but here she was baring herself to a man she'd known only three days. Exceptional days, but a short span of hours nonetheless.

"I think your bright mind and honest character have assessed the situation candidly and accurately, but your heart still feels like that little girl watching her daddy walk away."

Lauren squeezed her lips and her eyelids together, holding it in with every fiber of her will, but a sob escaped her. Hot tears traced twin paths to her chin.

"I'm such an idiot!" She scrubbed at her face with her fists. "Why should it matter after all these years?"

Kent tossed his fishing pole aside, and his warm arms wrapped around her.

"If it had ceased to matter," Kent spoke, his deep voice in her ear, "you wouldn't be the wonderful, caring person you are. You guard your heart, but it's not calloused, and it's anything but hard. Huge difference. I don't think I've ever met anyone quite like you, Jade Eyes."

Then she was laughing and crying at the same time into the scruffy fur collar of his bomber jacket. The jacket smelled like him and like their time here together—earthy sweat and pine and smoke. If she could bottle the scent she'd make a mint. On second thought, she'd just keep it all for herself.

Whoa! What was she thinking? This man was not hers. He'd said nice things that made her feel better, but he was probably just sorry for her. She pulled away, and he let her go, fully proving her deduction.

"Thanks for your kindness and understanding," she said, keeping her face carefully averted. "What were some of those ideas you had for catching our saboteur?"

She couldn't look up. Facing the pity in his eyes would hurt too much.

Kent's heart squeezed in his chest. Why did she do that all the time—get close and then pull away? Why did he care? He already knew there was no romantic future for them after this crisis passed. If only he could stop wishing that weren't true. But he couldn't turn back the clock and unlearn his lesson about meddling mamas—as charming as Lauren's might be.

Okay, if Lauren could tuck her emotions away and get down to business, so could he. In a few terse sentences, he explained what he had in mind.

She actually bought into it, and the weight

in his gut lightened. They might be nuts—certifiable!—but they were really going to do this. Desperate times and all that.

He ought to be discouraged, since they had caught no fish, and he'd also deduced that the beavers were gone from the valley, too—probably fat and sassy from consuming every last fish in their pond prior to departure. One less source of nourishment for the survivors.

At the stream's edge, they scored some cattail roots and red clover to supplement their diet, but scrounging up enough food for the winter was not a priority. In fact, it was a pipe dream. If they hoped to survive, they had to get out of this valley and back to civilization... soon. Now he and Lauren had made a plan to identify the scum who must be hiding his means of escape until after he'd eliminated everyone else.

As Lauren pointed out while they fine-tuned their strategy, "Whoever this guy is, he wouldn't kill us all off and then leave himself to starve. He must have a way to get out of here. Something he's hiding from the rest of us."

Truly, Lauren possessed a cutting-edge mind. He couldn't disagree with her even as his thoughts cast around for ideas on what that way might be. Whatever it was, the guy would have to give it up after they captured him. Kent had a few devious thoughts on how the lowlife could be induced to talk, and no one would have to lay a finger on the creep.

With their meager booty, Kent and Lauren hurried side-by-side back toward the mercantile.

"What's that noise?" She grabbed his arm and halted him.

Kent's gaze locked with hers as they listened. Screaming…no, more like yelling, then a crash, along with the sound of splintering wood.

"They're under attack at the mercantile!"

Heart hammering, Kent broke into a sprint with Lauren on his heels. He bounded onto the front porch in one leap just in time to catch the distinctive thud of fist meeting flesh. A pained outcry greeted him as he rushed over the threshold, weapon drawn, and took in the situation in a split-second glance.

The place was a mess—water bottles and foodstuffs strewn about, shelving toppled, the couch from the plane upended, Nina pale as a sheet and pressed against the wall, but most alarming, the cluster of red-faced men surrounding a single, cowering figure. Fists drew back to continue pummeling their victim. Kent lifted his gun toward the open doorway and fired a shot into the empty street. The report reverberated around the room. Everyone froze.

"What is going on in here?" Kent barked.

"Oh, thank God, you've come back," Nina cried out, tears streaming down her face. She rushed to Lauren, who stood at Kent's side. "Dirk made a jerk of himself one too many times, and the guys decided he was the one trying to kill us, and…and…" She swept a hand toward the furious mob.

Lauren grasped her mother in a hug as the woman softly sobbed. Her tight-lipped gaze at Kent demanded action. He offered an infinitesimal nod and stepped toward the combatants.

"Back off, everyone, and get a grip."

"This is the guy," Cliff pronounced, hands still fisted.

Dirk dropped to the floor in a tight ball and lay shuddering.

"He admitted it," said Rich, gesturing fiercely toward Dirk with one crutch.

"What exactly did he say?"

The vengeful attackers—Cliff, Rich and Neil—looked from one to another without a word. A throat cleared, and Kent spied Phil sitting against one wall, massaging the calf above his injured foot.

The man scowled toward the interrupted melee. "These jokers nearly crushed me beneath the toppled shelving. If I hadn't already been scooting out of the way, I'd be nursing a bunch more injuries."

Cliff's gaze lowered toward his toes, and Neil backed away from the man on the floor, shaking his head like he was waking himself up from a bad dream.

"Aw, man," said Rich, "we really weren't thinking."

"I second that." Nina's tone could have frosted an iceberg.

"None of you have answered my question." Kent's gaze dissected first one and then another. Red faces turned pale.

Neil let out a long huff. "Our resident jerk said he'd be happy to leave our rotting carcasses behind in this godforsaken valley."

Kent glared down at Dirk, who was starting to unroll from his snail-like huddle. "Stupid thing to say."

"And mean-spirited," Lauren added.

"But it sounds more like the Dirk we all know and dislike rather than an admission of guilt."

Dirk lifted his head. His lower face and neck were covered in blood that continued to drip from his misshapen nose.

A wordless exclamation came from Lauren. "Looks like it's broken. I'll have to set it as best I can."

"I'b pressing charges on these baniacs as sood as we get back to cibilization," Dirk announced, his nasal impairment evident as he sat up.

With glares all around at the man's attackers, Lauren knelt in front of him.

"Let's get this place back in order," Kent said, and the able-bodied scurried to comply.

Soon Lauren's infirmary was restored, and her new patient was stretched out beside Phil with his nose taped, sleeping under the influence of one of Rich's painkillers.

Kent joined her where she knelt at Dirk's side. "Does he have any other injuries?"

She rose and met his gaze. Those jade eyes were dark and deeply troubled.

"Bruised ribs where Rich's crutch whapped him a good one and a sore stomach where Neil's fist connected. The broken nose was all Cliff. These people are on the ragged edge of insanity, and I don't entirely blame them."

"Me either." He lowered his voice. "Is Operation Eagle a go?"

Her chin dipped a strong affirmative. Gutsy lady. Kent grinned. This afternoon was going to be very interesting…or very boring, if their quarry refused to rise to the bait.

Half an hour later, Kent was situated on the wide ledge where he had rescued Lauren a few hours earlier—an eagle's nest where he could watch everything that happened down below. Everyone thought he'd gone out to hunt for late-season dandelions, which were edible in almost every part of the plant. Instead, he gazed down at the frontier town with his binoculars.

As soon as Lauren played her crucial part, he might expect to spot illicit activity. Earlier, she hadn't been able to identify with the naked eye the person who was up to no good, but the binoculars would expose the culprit. Then they could apply the appropriate pressure to get answers. At this point, not many holds were barred in that endeavor.

Kent turned and gave his perch a long study. The mystery dweller had showed up here and in an alley down in the town—both times apparently stalking Lauren. If Kent had hackles, they'd be standing at attention at the mere thought of some crazy mountain man getting his hands on her. This time she was safe—relatively speaking—at the mercantile, which was why Kent had taken the role of the eagle and had made sure his sidearm was ready with a round chambered. The guy could possibly be nuts, but his uncanny ability to remain hidden showed he wasn't stupid. It would be senseless for him to attack a full-grown, armed man. Kent would be surprised if he had anything to worry about in regard to the mystery dweller.

He settled down on the ledge cross-legged and surveyed his domain with the binoculars. The magnifying lenses brought the cliff sides into focus, and he spotted several areas that must have been mine entrances, but his earlier assumption had been confirmed. They had been dynamited shut. Too bad. Despite the risks of exploring the ancient tunnels, one or more of the mine shafts may have led to the other side of the mountain and a way out of this valley.

Kent returned his scrutiny to the town. Nothing stirred yet. That couldn't last long with the bombshell Lauren was about to explode oh-so-innocently in the midst of the survivors.

Kent grinned. This was almost fun.

A soft sound came from behind him—a pebble displacing. Kent began to turn but something hard as a baseball bat collided with his head. Hot pain engulfed his skull. Then nothing.

TEN

"Don't get too frisky," Lauren admonished Rich as he restlessly crutched around the room, putting more and more weight on his injured knee. "Let those muscles and ligaments heal."

She took a sip of the tea her mother had prepared for her. The refreshing warmth slid down her throat. If only she could truly let her guard down and take a rest break. She ordered herself to present a relaxed figure as she leaned back into the airplane seat. By now, Kent should have reached his perch and commenced his eagle-eyed watch. Time to bait the trap and see who stepped into it.

Cliff slouched a couple of seats down from her, expression gloomy and morose. Dirk and Phil still lay in the infirmary, but judging by the murmur of conversation from that area, they were awake and conversing and would be able to hear anything she said. Neil lay flopped across the couch with one arm over his eyes, but his breathing said he wasn't asleep. The prevailing atmosphere was utter hopelessness. Yet, someone among them hoped for everyone else to die and for himself to escape to civilization.

Why did this person need wholesale death and destruction? In order for his current identity to disappear from the face of the earth? She had discussed this possibility—no, probability—with Kent. It was the only solution that made sense. Whoever wanted the plane to crash, also wanted no one to be looking for them forevermore. They would be presumed dead.

Mom settled into the seat next to Lauren and patted her knee. "We'll be okay for a couple of days with the provisions we have. I might even try my hand at making biscuits with the flour, lard and baking powder we retrieved in that last load before the hut burned. I make no promises about how they'll turn out, but—" She shrugged eloquently.

"Sounds good, Mom."

"You seem a million miles away, dear."

"Just asking myself useless questions, like how we happened to be on this doomed flight. Is our presence merely coincidental?"

Mom's eyes popped wide. "What else could it be? Who would want to kill you and me?"

"That's the dilemma, all right."

Neil sat up on his elbow, gaze fixed earnestly on them. "Dear ladies, I cannot imagine why anyone would want to deprive the world of your presences."

Mom giggled, a coy little sound, and Lauren gave her a sidelong look. *Sheesh!* Flattery got a person everywhere with her mother. On the flip side, Lauren's scam antennae always went up, which was hardly fair to the person delivering the compliment. Give someone the benefit of the doubt for once, she scolded herself.

"On the good news side of things," she said, allowing herself to smile, "Kent thinks there might be a way to beam a communication signal out of this valley."

Cliff went stiff and straight. "But the radio is broken."

"I'm not talking about the two-way radio. There's a satellite phone in a cubby on the plane."

Dirk stalked out of the infirmary, the white bandage on his nose a sharp contrast to his red face. "Why didn't he come up with this sooner?"

"Because a sat phone is even more sensitive to the iron ore deposits in this valley than a radio or the airplane black box, but it might be able to connect with a satellite if he can climb the cliffs higher than we were yesterday."

"Faint hope," Rich muttered.

"Better than no hope," Neil countered.

Lauren lowered her eyes. She couldn't afford to have anyone read a hint of intrigue in them. Everything she had said was true…as far as it went. There was a sat phone in the plane, but Kent had checked it during one of his trips back and forth with people and supplies, and someone had removed the batteries.

The battery thief was likely Mags prior to their departure, but Lauren and Kent were hoping against hope that this little detail was not known to her accomplice. Sabotaging the sat phone was mute testimony from the copilot that she thought there was an off-chance her skilled pilot might actually land the plane after the bomb went off. As they'd laid their plans, Kent had told Lauren he could do without such backhanded tributes.

Now that the bait had been laid out, it only remained to be seen which of them made an excuse to leave the mercantile to stop Kent from trying the satellite phone. Kent would be watching and waiting from his perch to spot such suspicious activity.

Time ticked along, and Mom hummed as

she got busy on her biscuits. Neil went outside to get fresh air but came back within a couple of minutes. Cliff did the same and then he and Neil gave Phil a hand with the same chore. Pretty soon everyone had been out and come in, except for Lauren and her mother, but no one was gone long enough to make an attempt to seek out Kent. Lauren hid a scowl. Their ploy might be going bust.

Hours passed, and a plate of rather chewy biscuits was passed around, along with a few more strips of jerky. Neil, Cliff and a resentful Dirk left to collect another bucket of water.

"Did you catch a glimpse of Kent?" Lauren ventured when they returned in twenty minutes with a full bucket. Nothing suspicious about that timing.

The men shook their heads. Alarm jangled in Lauren's chest. Kent should have been back by now. They'd decided he would hang up the surveillance by supper time if no suspects presented themselves.

"My turn for some fresh air." She stood up.

"I'll go with you," Mom said.

They made their way to the alley behind the mercantile, and Lauren halted her mother with a hand on her arm.

"Kent and I were running a fishing expedition for our saboteur this afternoon, but nobody took the bait and went after him. He should have been back by now. I'm worried."

Mom's brow puckered. "There's no satellite phone?"

"There is, but it's not in working order. We were hoping the killer wouldn't know that and would make a play to stop Kent from using it."

"We should get a search party together and look for him. We can't lose our hero pilot."

"No, I—we can't."

"Do I detect more than a hint of personal interest?" Mom's face lit.

"Don't get your hopes up. Go back in and send Neil and Cliff out. I'll take them to where Kent was supposed to be, and we'll go from there."

"I'll come with you."

"You need to stay here and mind the store. Especially keep an eye on Dirk. He's more or less in decent shape, and he's among our prime suspects—one of the three executives from Peerless One. If Dirk tries anything, have Rich clobber him with one of his crutches."

Her dainty mother delivered a downright feral grin. "Will do. And watch out for Cliff. He's strong again and is also a Peerless One executive."

"But Cliff almost died from narcotics slipped into his coffee."

"How do we know he didn't dose his own coffee…or even take the drugs in pill form washed down by his coffee? What better mask of innocence than an attempt on his own life? Methinks our saboteur enjoys risk—dancing on the edge. He was counting on Dirk to find him within a half hour of ingesting the pills and counting on you to save him medically. Dirk failed him, but you didn't."

Lauren's jaw dropped then she let out a small chuckle. "Mother! You have a more devious mind than I do, if that's possible."

"But I could be right."

"You could, indeed. Please, send the guys out."

A few minutes later, she was trudging out of Trouble Creek, Cliff flanking her on one side and Neil on the other. The sensation of potential threat on either side was unpleasant to say the least. By the time they passed the wrecked plane, the sun was leaning hard into the mountain ridges that soared up beyond their imprisoning valley. They would have to hurry.

Abruptly, Neil let out a yelp and collapsed onto the ground. A few not-nice words escaped his lips as he massaged his ankle. "Some critter dug a hole in the ground, and I stepped in it. Twisted my ankle."

"Can you walk?"

Neil rose and made the attempt, but stumbled with a whimper. Cliff grabbed him and held him upright while Lauren knelt and pulled up the man's pants leg to eyeball the ankle.

"Possible mild swelling, but it's early. A sprain will continue to swell and become more painful as time goes on." She rose and looked at Cliff. "You'll have to get him back to the mercantile as quickly as you can. Then haul in some ice water, and let him soak the ankle. My mother can wrap it after the soak."

Cliff shook his head. "You need to come back with us."

"Not going to happen. I know where Kent was going, and I intend to find him before dark."

"Your mother will have our scalps," Neil protested.

"She, more than anyone on the planet, knows how stubborn I can be. But to stay on the safe side, don't let her lay hands on the hatchet."

Cliff snorted a laugh, as he turned a groaning Neil back toward town.

As Lauren watched them go, a long sigh shuddered through her. Another name on the injured list. *Please God, don't let me find Kent injured, too, or— Stop!* She couldn't let her mind go in the direction of worse than hurt. He was fine. He had to be! Hopefully, she'd meet him returning to the mercantile. Any minute now…

Kent's awareness floated in and out of focus. One moment his senses registered heat washing over his front side, cold against his back and intermittent snapping, crackling sounds. The next who-knew-how-many moments faded into oblivion.

Where was he? How long had he been here? Why did his head hurt? The questions flitted through his brain like moths that refused to light upon anything solid.

Finally, a semblance of coherent thought gelled. Someone had clobbered him. That's why his head hurt. Those snapping sounds were sap-filled branches burning. He seemed to be within a few feet of the fire, which was why his front side felt warm and his back chilled. He lay on a hard surface, and his muscles ached. Time to open his eyes and figure out where he'd been taken, but his eyelids rebelled against his will. Consciousness faded again.

Scents awoke him—piney smell from the fire—metallic dankness—an overlaying stink like dead animal mingled with human body odor. His eyelids flew wide then winced shut at the brilliance of the flames a few feet from his face. He opened his eyes to slits and studied as much of his environment as he could take in. His body ached to stir and stretch, but his sense that he was not alone held him still.

The uneven rock walls surrounding him were that of a cave, which he could see was strewn with assorted belongings of a human variety. A pickax and a shovel rested against the nearest wall. A metal mug rested on a rock beside an old-fashioned coffeepot. Dented pots and pans, some containing crusted remains of food, cluttered the perimeter of the fire. Kent's stomach growled even as his gorge rose, and he tasted bile on his tongue.

Tentatively, he lifted his head. Pain shot through his skull, and stars spangled his vision. An involuntary groan left his lips.

A guttural cackle answered his pained noise. Kent struggled onto one elbow, and discovered his hands were bound together in front of him with strips of tanned leather. His gaze found a pair of dirty boots standing a few feet away. Above the boots a pair of filthy jeans led past stocky knees to an uneven row of gopher and squirrel tails sewn around the hem of a coat made of many animal pelts. The unpleasant stench was coming from the coat and the unwashed man beneath it. Kent's neck ached as he craned his head upward to take in the mountain of a man. Inky eyes stared back at him set into a face framed by a tangled mat of deep brown hair and beard. Thick, red lips frowned down at him.

Firelight glinted off a shiny object, and Kent dropped his gaze to the bowie knife the mountain man gripped in beefy fingers. His captor grunted and motioned with his knife that Kent should stand up.

Gritting his teeth, Kent managed to get to his knees without tipping over. His slow and sloppy response evidently strained his captor's patience. The man grasped his shirt in a massive fist and hauled him upright then half carried, half dragged him to a spot on the cave wall where he hooked Kent's bound wrists over a natural protrusion. Kent's knees buckled, sending pain through his arms and cramping his lungs. He forced his legs to stiffen and hold his weight.

His captor waved the knife back and forth in front of Kent's face. Slowly, the unnaturally red lips peeled back, exposing blackened teeth. Rank animal breath assaulted Kent's nose. He turned his head away, but the mountain man gripped his chin and forced his gaze forward. Bizarre noises that sounded nothing like words began to leave the man's mouth.

A strangling sensation gripped Kent's throat as he gazed into his captor's maw. The man's tongue was a stump, and what passed for lips was little more than scar tissue. Something horrible had been done to this guy. Was that what had driven him into a hermetic existence in the mountains?

The man tried again to form words, but Kent shook his head. His captor threw his arms up and let out a cry that communicated frustration and anger. He stomped over to a crate sitting nearby and picked up a thin, black square and a stump of what appeared to be chalk.

Silence descended, except for the occasional snap of the fire and the hiss of chalk across the miniature blackboard. At last, the mountain man finished his painstaking message, strode back to Kent, and thrust the board nearly into his face.

"Woman come here for you," Kent read aloud.

He lifted his gaze to the pair of flat, black eyes that locked with his over the top edge of the board. His captor lowered the chalkboard, exposing a wide grin. Tentacles of ice wrapped around Kent's heart. He'd been in a lot of tough spots during his tours of duty, but any fear he experienced then paled before this moment. This filthy brute was using him as bait to capture Lauren!

Heat flared in his chest. He leaped upward, freeing his bound hands from the rock, and lunged for his captor. The man's ham fist connected with Kent's chin, and his teeth snapped together. White-hot shards of pain sliced through his head as his back slammed into the stone wall. His legs buckled, and unholy laughter faded in his ears as he descended into a pit of nothingness.

ELEVEN

Lauren struggled to concentrate as she climbed the cliff face toward the ledge. Something was definitely wrong. There was no way Kent would still be sitting up there, watching. Not after he must have seen her trudging toward his lookout spot.

At last, she pulled herself up onto the ledge. Her mouth went dry as her gaze hunted frantically for him. He was no longer here. She scanned the valley. Nothing moved below. The sun was cradled between a pair of mountain peaks and settling lower every moment. She couldn't remain here long before heading back. It was out of the question to be in the open alone after dark.

No sign of Kent on the ledge. Or was there?

She knelt and studied the rock. A pair of faint parallel scuff marks led toward the rock face behind the ledge, as if something—or someone—had been dragged. The mystery dweller must have gotten Kent! But where did the mountain man take him? No way did the guy carry Kent off this ledge, either up or down. Not physically possible.

Following the intermittent drag marks, she came to the cliff side, and the marks disappeared into a blank rock wall. Sort of.

Heart pounding, Lauren sidled to the right, and there it was—a crack in the rock just wide enough for a person to slip through. Staring at the cliff straight on, she couldn't have seen the crack because one side of the entrance folded over the other. The opening had to be approached obliquely in order for it to be noticed. And what was more, in the growing dusk, an unnatural light glowed from within.

Was this cave the mystery dweller's lair? Goose bumps prickled over Lauren's flesh. No wonder he had been able to slink up behind her, startling her into tumbling off the ledge. He'd no doubt sneaked up on Kent also. The creepy guy must have taken Kent into the cave. Was he hurt? Was he even still alive?

She should go back and get help, but the only able-bodied people available were her mother and Cliff. She wasn't going to bring her mother up here, and doing anything alone with Cliff would be foolish. It was looking more and more like he was the saboteur who got them here in the first place. That left only her, and if Kent needed help, she was all over it.

Lauren stepped into the cave. The walls continued close for several paces, and then widened gradually to six feet apart or so. A gamy, smoky smell grew stronger the farther she went and so did the flickering illumination. Fire, no doubt. A sudden snap as of burning wood bore out that deduction. Lauren hardly dared breathe as she crept forward. No other sounds warned her of what she might find ahead. Was the mystery dweller lying in wait for her?

Abruptly, one side of the passage came to an end, and a space like a large room opened before her. She stood stock-still and scanned the area. At the center, a fire crackled in a rock-encircled fire pit. A few pots and pans lay to the side of the pit next to a ragged and stained camp chair. No one perched in the seat. On the far wall, a variety of animal skins hung from a line, plus a pair of dingy white socks at the far end, ludicrously out of place. To the left, a variety of foodstuffs occupied a large set of shelves, reminiscent of the shelving in the burned hut. To the right against the wall lay a bundle of furs. A face poked out from the bundle. Kent's face!

Lauren hurried to him and knelt at his side. Drying blood spread from above his ear down the side of his face and disappeared at his neckline. The head wound didn't appear to be bleeding further, and his breathing was regular, but his eyes were closed, and he lay inert. She pulled the furs away from him and discovered his hands were bound. She needed to get him loose.

"Kent," she said softly as she struggled with the tight knot. "Please wake up. We've got to get out of here. Kent!"

A groan and a mumble answered her. Kent's body stirred.

"C'mon, honey, wake u-u-u-up."

His eyes popped open, and he winced, but a rather loopy grin appeared. "Honey?"

"You're imagining things," she snapped. How did that endearment slip out? No time to examine her own lunacy now.

Awareness abruptly sharpened Kent's gaze. "Leave me. Get out of here! Now!" He lifted his head as his gaze sprang wide on a spot over her shoulder. "Too late! Look out, Lauren!"

A guttural growl sounded behind her, and every hair on her body stood to attention.

Slowly, she rose and turned. Something between a squeak and a gasp left her tightened throat.

A hulking brute from somebody's worst nightmare stepped out of the shadows and blocked the cave exit. He was covered in furs from knee to neck, and a fur hood shrouded his head with the tail of some critter dangling down to his nose. No wonder she'd mistaken him for a bizarre animal in the glimpse she'd had of him before she tumbled from the ledge. His inky stare froze her in place, and she didn't dare to move a muscle.

"Where…is…your…gun?" she half whispered to Kent, who was struggling to gain his feet.

"I don't know. It's not on me. He must have it."

What the creature held in front of him was not a firearm, but a massive knife that glinted, sharp and deadly, in the light of flickering flames. He let out a grunt and motioned toward the fire with the knife. Lauren edged in that direction in a slow shuffle, gaze fixed on the hulking menace.

If he charged her, where should she go? His presence blocked the exit to the outdoors. And even if she got past him, she was likely to take a fatal tumble trying to climb down the side of the cliff faster than a guy who'd lived here indefinitely.

"Keep the fire between you and him," Kent said in low tones.

Out of the corner of her eye, she caught him working with his teeth at the bonds around his hands. If he got loose, she'd have help, but would it be soon enough?

Their captor was motioning insistently for her to sit in the ratty camp chair. She shook her head so hard her ponytail whipped her face. Become stationary so he could grab her? Not hardly. She continued to back away, and he let out a deep growl. Her flesh crawled.

"Let's talk about this," she said, lifting her hands, palms out. "We mean you no harm." Too bad the sentiment didn't seem to be mutual. "Can you help us get out of this valley? We'll go away and leave you alone."

He responded with a slash of his knife and a leap toward her. Kent yelled and lunged to his feet, continuing to struggle with the leather ties. Lauren screamed and backpedaled, heart hammering. She tripped over something and sprawled onto her back, pain spiraling through her torso. The mountain man was almost upon her when Kent hit him in a full body slam, and they tumbled to the ground a few feet away.

"Run, Lauren!" Kent hollered.

Their assailant let out a roar and raised his knife. Still on her back, Lauren kicked at him with all her might. She connected with his ear. He howled, rolling away from Kent and clutching the side of his face with one hand. Unfortunately, the knife remained fisted in his other hand.

Kent wobbled up onto his elbows and knees, shaking his head. Lauren scrambled to him and pulled at his arm.

"Up you go, big guy!"

"Get out of here!" His gaze shot fire as he shoved her away and turned toward the mountain man who was lunging to his feet.

She staggered back, and a slight chill caressed her cheek. Glancing toward the source of the chill, her eyes widened. A passageway! Without a second thought, she darted into it. Since this guy was fixated on her, maybe he wouldn't stop to stick his knife into Kent before he came after her.

The passage was cool and slightly dank. The light from the cavern room illuminated only a short way into the passage. The walls looked like natural rock, not hewn out by man, so this was not part of an old mine. Where it would lead was another question. The trajectory appeared to be slightly upward along an uneven floor.

Lauren fumbled in her pocket for her phone. Just before the pitch darkness swallowed her, she punched on the flashlight app. If only the light wasn't going to lead her pursuer right to her, but the alternative was perhaps tumbling down some sinkhole. Getting lost in the bowels of the earth was also a probability if passages started branching off this one. On the other hand, if she could find a place to hide or a way to double back, that would be priceless.

She strained to pick up on noises behind her, but she could hardly hear for the pounding of her pulse in her ears. The lack of sound was more than ominous. What was happening back there? Was Kent still among the living? Her insides cramped, squeezing tears to her eyes. She blinked them away.

Get a grip. She had to keep a cool head and fight smart, or she might never again see the light of day.

Kent struggled for consciousness. He must have blacked out again. But for how long? The fire-lit room appeared empty of human inhabitants. Where had Lauren and their attacker gone? For that matter, why was he still alive? The man mountain could easily have knifed him and eliminated any threat he posed, which, as weak as he felt right now, wasn't much.

He lifted himself up on one elbow, and the leather straps around his wrists loosened. Between Lauren's efforts and his own, the knot must have come undone. He shook off the bonds and pulled himself to his feet, using handholds on the rock wall.

His head pounded as he squinted around the room and listened for telltale sounds. He took a step toward the exit from the cave, but pulled up short as a muffled scrape came from the opposite direction. Turning, he spotted a passage at the back of the cave. Lauren had gone in there? Not unlikely, since the knife-wielding hulk had been between her and the great outdoors.

If he was going to overcome the giant he would need a weapon. His gun did not appear in evidence, but the pickax leaning against the wall was a lot better than nothing. Besides, it had a significantly longer reach than the other guy's knife. Grabbing the ax, he headed for the passage into the mountain.

As much as his feet longed to hurry toward Lauren, he proceeded with caution, stopping to listen every few feet. His own breathing was so loud he probably wouldn't hear anyone else's.

But then came a stuttering thump like someone maybe tripping and catching themselves.

Reassured that he was on the right trail, Kent continued but soon had to dig his phone from his pocket and turn on the flashlight. Lauren would surely be using her phone app to provide light for her feet, but how was her pursuer gaining illumination? Since no light showed ahead, he clearly wasn't close enough to either of them to find out. He quickened his pace. If the mystery dweller had not caught up to Lauren yet, he could at any moment, and Kent needed to be there to thwart the guy—or die trying.

Both Lauren and he were at a great disadvantage, because this guy likely knew the passage like the back of his hand. This was his territory, and they were the newcomers...and the prey. *God, help us.* The simple prayer had never held more urgency.

The passage meandered a bit, but so far remained single, which on the one hand was a good thing. No chance of getting lost in a maze. On the other hand, it was a bad thing. No chance of confusing their enemy or even of doubling back.

Abruptly, the passage widened into a cavern smaller than the one that served as the mountain man's dwelling. Apparently, this was his storage area. Half a dozen long, narrow crates and three large wooden barrels hugged the walls. Near those stood a makeshift furnace and a set of bar-shaped molds. Kent passed his light over the containers. No markings indicated the contents, but the lid was ajar on one of the barrels. He hazarded a peek inside. Empty.

Or maybe not. Something glinted at him from the bottom. He reached in and picked up a weighty gold coin. A buffalo looked back at him on one side and a Native American on the other. He let out a low whistle. If he was not mistaken, this was a very valuable coin. By the weight it had to be pure gold—at least an ounce. He glanced back toward the furnace and molds. Was the cave dweller melting down coins and transforming them into bars?

His mind spun with a whole new gamut of possible motives for why his plane was sabotaged in this exact area. One seemed most likely. Somebody in their party knew of this bizarre mountain man, where he was holed up and what was hidden in his cave. The saboteur had intended to parachute down into this area all along. The deduction was solid, because greed and crime were best buddies.

He shook his head and filed the knowledge away. No time to investigate further or even allow himself to get distracted from the primary goal—protecting Lauren.

Unfortunately, two passages led away from this small grotto. Kent stepped into one of them and listened. Silence greeted him. He went into the other one, and a distant clink like a kicked stone met his ears. How close was he to catching up? He shut off his flashlight app and strained his eyes. Hopefully, he wasn't imagining things but a faint glow seemed to beckon him onward.

Kent turned on his light and quickened his pace, or at least tried to. This passage was rougher than the last, and the uneven flooring—sometimes dipping or rising abruptly almost like a stair step—kept slowing him down. It seemed like he'd been walking through the interior of the mountain forever. Could be a mile. Could be two. Or, for all he knew, in his half-disoriented state, it might only have been a few hundred feet.

A familiar beep from his phone sent an icy shock to his gut. The battery was dying. He had to catch up to his quarry soon or be left in the dark where a misstep could tumble him into a neck-breaking fall.

The glow ahead was growing stronger. His heart rate ramped up a notch. He was making up the distance. If only he could get to their attacker before the hulk got to Lauren. Kent tightened his grip on the ax handle.

A scream echoed up the passageway. Lauren!

Discarding all caution, Kent broke into a run. *Please God, don't let me be too late!*

TWELVE

Lauren had done what she most desperately had not wanted to do—tumbled into a hole. That's what came of forging ahead while looking back over her shoulder. At least it wasn't a terribly deep hole, as evidenced by the fact that she was still alive and relatively unhurt, except for scraped palms and knees, and assorted bumps and bruises.

No doubt her involuntary shriek had alerted her pursuer that she was in trouble. Not good. Not good at all. A shiver coursed up her spine. She sat very still in the dark, listening for him, but the rasp of her own breathing could easily be masking the telltale sounds of his approach.

Her cell had flown from her fingers, and its light abruptly extinguished. Did that mean it was broken or just that the app had triggered off? Not that the answer mattered if she couldn't find it again. Yet she was obliged to try.

Still on her hands and knees, she began groping the area. No phone, but she did come across a decent-sized rock. She fisted her hand around it, liking the heft and its sharp edges. The story of David and Goliath moved front and center in her mind. She'd only get one throw, but that was all David had needed. A prayer whispered from her heart.

Was she imagining things, or had a faint glow begun growing from the direction she had come? She suppressed her breathing, but could do nothing about the thunder of her pulse in her ears. Yes, a light was growing brighter. Was she imagining grunted breathing and the slap of footfalls? No, she was not. Ignoring twinges of pain from her skinned knees and bruised muscles, Lauren drew herself up tall.

One throw. Make it good!

Then she saw him. In the light of a kerosene lamp he held in one hand, the brute was every bit as fearsome as she remembered. A tremor coursed through her. He stopped at the edge of the pit she'd fallen into. Lauren kept her focus on her adversary, but her peripheral vision noted that she hadn't actually tumbled into a hole. More like she'd stepped over a drop-off, and another one—who knew how deep—loomed only a few yards to her right, while the passage continued to her left.

Lifting her rock into throwing position, Lauren backed slowly in the direction of the passage. The fur-covered mountain man halted at the edge of the drop-off, and his maimed lips drew back in a chilling grin. Lauren's skin crawled.

"Stay back!" She'd intended to speak firmly, boldly, but the words emerged in a raspy whisper.

A deep rumble came from the hulk's barrel chest. Laughter! He didn't take her seriously. Her insides shriveled. How could she blame him? In this situation, she barely took *herself* seriously.

The mountain man stepped off the ledge and landed with solid grace on her level. He now stood scarcely ten feet from her, still grinning and holding his knife. His rank smell invaded Lauren's nostrils, turning her stomach. Lifting the lamp high, he took a stride toward her.

Lauren threw, aiming for his head, just like David. The rock connected with the kerosene lamp. Glass shattered. Kerosene flew, much of it splashing her assailant. The flaming wick hit the man's fur coat and ignited the accelerant. In an instant, the man was a human torch.

Backpedaling, Lauren threw one arm up, shielding her face from the heat, but she could not tear her eyes from the horrific sight. Shrieking and flapping his arms like a wounded vulture, he staggered first this way and then that.

"Drop and roll!" Lauren cried. "Drop and roll!"

Her life-saving words appeared not to register as the man seemed determined to extinguish the flames by slapping at them with his bare hands. It was a losing battle. The greasy, matted hair and beard and filthy furs were ready fuel for hungry fire. Still shrieking and slapping at himself, the mountain man reached the edge of the other drop-off and tumbled over. Long seconds passed, and a solid thump terminated the piercing screams.

Silence and darkness reigned. Lauren lost what little food remained in her stomach. How could she ever scrub this horrible memory from her mind? And yet, her faulty aim had worked its purpose. Her pursuer could not hurt her now. She should be thankful, and she was, but mostly she felt sick. Now, she was alone in the heart of the mountain with no light to guide her out.

Her back was to the rock wall. Eyes squeezed

tightly shut, she slid down it into a hunched crouch and let the sobs come.

"Lauren."

Her heart tripped over itself. *Oh, great! Could things get any worse?* Now she was hallucinating voices.

"Lauren!"

The urgency of the tone stabbed through her, and her eyes popped open. She was no longer in the dark, but the light was faint. Looking up, she found a panting Kent standing on the lip of the drop-off with his lit phone in one hand and a pickax in the other. He was disheveled, dirty and the most wonderful thing she'd ever seen. Wincing, he released the pickax, sat down on the ledge and let himself drop the rest of the way. She rose and ran to him. His arms closed around her, and she burrowed into him, babbling like a crazy woman about a rock, and Goliath, and fire, and falling.

Gradually, she managed to let him know exactly what happened. She lifted her head, expecting to see shock and horror on his face for her confession about setting a man on fire.

Instead, his gaze held tenderness, and he laid a finger across her lips. "Shhh," he said. "I'm here now."

Sniffling, she stepped back and examined

him. How foolish for her to be bawling when he was the one who had been brutally attacked. Pain lines bracketed his mouth, and dried blood streaked one side of his face.

"You're hurt," she said. "We need to get you back to the mercantile."

"I don't think so. My phone is about to go dead, and I'm too exhausted to feel my way back down this passage."

Lauren cast her gaze around, searching for her phone. She spotted it a few feet away and scooped it up. The screen was shattered, and it did not awaken to her touch. Her teeth ground together. What could go wrong next?

As if to answer her question, Kent's phone went dark. She reached out, found Kent's chest and fisted her fingers in his shirt.

"We have to get out of here."

"I know." He sighed. "Just let me rest a little while."

He slumped to the ground, and she settled in beside him.

"I can't let you fall asleep," she said. "You probably have a concussion."

"Seems to be an epidemic of that around here." He chuckled, but the sound broke off into a soft whine.

"Your head hurts?"

"Like a sharp-beaked woodpecker is going to town inside my brain."

Lauren nestled closer to him, and his arm went around her shoulder. Deep contentment soothed the turbulence of her pulse.

"You know," she said. "I should still be terrified, trapped in a cave with no illumination and no supplies, but I'm not. You do that to me—make me feel safe. I'm not used to that sensation, especially with a guy."

Kent tucked her head under his chin. "Glad I can be of service. Sorry I arrived too late to clobber the man mountain, but you handled yourself like a champ."

"Man mountain?"

"You know how I attach nicknames. He was a mountain of a man."

She stiffened. "What if he's still alive down there…in pain…we—"

"—can't help him, darlin'. It's okay not to take responsibility for the wounds of the world. Besides, not only was he a very bad man who tried to hurt my very favorite good person in the world, I think he was in on this whole setup with whoever sabotaged the plane."

Lauren sat up straight. Which order of business did she address first? Him calling her his favorite good person—words that sent warm fuzzies through her middle—or his statement that the Neanderthal who tried to attack her could possibly be linked to the person who caused their plane to crash-land?

"I discovered something pretty shocking back along the passage," he said. "I think the saboteur intended to end up in Trouble Creek after jumping out of the plane, but the bomb exploded prematurely, sending the whole planeload of us into the valley, rather than just him."

"And Mags," Lauren said.

"Yeah, Mags, too, but I doubt the mastermind behind the sabotage intended to let her live beyond her usefulness to him."

"What was it you found?"

"Do you remember passing through a room with some boxes and barrels in it?"

"Sure, but I didn't stop to investigate."

"I did. Briefly. The barrels likely held a whole bunch of gold coins like this one." He pressed a circular, flat object into her hand.

"Wow! This is heavy."

"No kidding. The cavern room also held a furnace and molds that could easily be used to melt the coins and form them into untraceable bars."

She let out a soft hum as a memory tickled her brain. "A few years ago, wasn't there a famous heist of newly minted gold buffalo-head coins? No one was ever arrested, and the coins disappeared without a trace."

"We may have stumbled across them— quite literally."

"We're still left with the question of who among the passengers is in on this deal."

"I know we've gone over this countless times, but do you remember anything—anything at all—from the time of the explosion that would give us a clue?"

Lauren sat very still and racked her brain for anything else she might have missed. "There is one thing."

"Go on."

"You said the cargo bay could be accessed from the bathroom. When the bomb went off, Dirk was in the bathroom. I remember looking back in that direction and seeing him lying half in and half out of the lavatory door."

"Dirk! Our least favorite guy."

"Circumstantial evidence, to borrow a legal phrase. Most recently, Cliff has been on the top of our suspect list."

"Our?"

"My mother's and mine. She came up with the hypothesis that Cliff drugged his own coffee to divert suspicion from himself, based on the understanding that Dirk would attempt to switch places with him in a half hour. Since I would be nearby to administer the antidote, he felt pretty confident of his survival, only it didn't work out quite as well as he intended, and he almost died."

"Devious deduction, but not out of the question."

Lauren shrugged. "That's my mother for you. Devious."

Kent went silent and still, almost as if he'd stopped breathing. Then a soft whistle came out from between his teeth.

"You know she's been her own worst enemy in her campaign to get me to fall in love with you."

Lauren's throat tightened. She already knew he didn't have those kinds of feelings for her. But worse, she wished he did. "I'm so sorry about that. She means well. You don't have to explain how off-putting it is though."

"I do have to explain. Six months ago, my heart got ripped out and trampled into the dirt by the woman of my dreams—or the woman I thought was my dream. I know now that I was delusional from the start, seeing what was never there in Elspeth. She wanted a supposedly dashing former Special Forces pilot on her elbow.

"In my mind, our relationship was serious.

In hers, I was a trophy. Sure, she'd wear my engagement ring for a while, but she never intended to let me get her up the aisle to say 'I do.' Not as long as her mother considered me unworthy of her precious daughter. It took me a long time—way too long for a normally intelligent man—to see reality. I swore I'd never allow myself to be taken in again by a woman under the thumb of a parent. When your mom started shoving us together, I assumed you fell into that category. I was wrong."

Kent's warm breath on her face told Lauren he was gazing straight at her. She could hardly trust herself to speak.

"In other words," she began in a raspy whisper, "my mother's machinations hindered matters, rather than helped."

"Let's just say, they created a smokescreen I've had a tough time seeing through."

A spurt of laughter left Lauren's lips. "I'm going to use that as ammo against her one of these days."

"With my blessing."

Lauren heard the grin in his tone.

"Now," he said, "if you'd be agreeable, I'm open to exploring the possibility that she might be right about us."

Happy tears spurted to the corners of Lauren's eyes. "I'll never tell her that."

"Me either. She'll have to see for herself."

Kent's mouth found hers—soft, warm, undemanding. Lauren allowed the kiss to linger, expecting that knee-jerk inner withdrawal that always came when a man tried to get close to her. Only peace remained, and that itself was just a little scary. She pulled away and leaned her head on his shoulder.

He cleared his throat. "Okay, so we still haven't one hundred percent deduced the identity of the saboteur."

Lauren was absurdly grateful for the change of subject. She had soul-searching to do in the area of lasting romance. This problem-solving was more comfortable right now.

She lifted her head. "I'm not sure how many more clues we can find until we somehow get back to the others."

Kent let out a low hum. "I have an odd question that may or may not lead anywhere."

"What is it?"

"Why would your stepfather tell your mother he knows me?"

"What do you mean?"

"When she was boarding the plane, she told me her husband vouched for me as a good guy. I assume that's why she was interested in me as relationship material for you. I've never seen or spoken to Marlin Barrington. Since he's got first dibs on the company jet, Peerless One only charters mine when other executives need to go a different direction than Barrington."

Lauren hugged her knees to her chest. "That *is* strange. Wait a sec! Mom told me that Marlin arranged personally for our trip to California, but that we were going to fly charter because the Peerless One jet was grounded for maintenance. I wonder if the company jet was really in the shop, or if Marlin didn't want to crash his own jet. Could he be a part of this?"

"You don't trust your stepfather much, do you?"

"Mom confessed to me that she's always had a weakness for bad boys. Even though Marlin appears solid gold on the outside, I've always sensed cheap brass on the inside. For my mom's sake, I've been trying to mark the reaction down to my chronic suspicion of the entire male race."

Kent let out a soft chuckle. "Maybe your instincts in this case are spot-on. But why kill you and his wife, and I still don't understand why he would tell your mother he knew me."

Lauren snorted. "That last part is easy. If Mom had the slightest inclination to forego the trip, a romantic prospect for me would seal the deal."

They batted ideas back and forth for a while, but conversation soon ebbed. Kent's nearness kept Lauren reasonably warm, but the utter blackness pressed in with a chill that had nothing to do with temperature. Her imagination saw more with her eyes closed than she could see with them open.

She yawned. "Don't fall asleep," she murmured to Kent.

"I won't," he murmured back.

Shivers drew Kent to consciousness. He was cold all over except his back where something warm pressed against him. Lauren! Kent gingerly sat up and confirmed that she was lying on her side with her back against his. Faint light bathed her feminine features and emphasized the darkness of her lashes against high cheekbones.

Light! Realization literally shook him, setting off a chain reaction of aches and pains from his head straight down to his toes. He ignored the discomfort. They were in the bowels of the mountain. There should be no illumination without a light source. This felt and looked like sunshine. Could they be near an opening to the outdoors?

Lauren let out a soft moan and opened

her eyes. Her gaze focused on him, and she smiled. Kent's heart did a backflip.

She gasped and sat up sharply. "We fell asleep! I'm so sorry! Are you all right?"

Her hands fluttered up and cupped his cheeks. Those jade eyes searched his face, sending a buoyant sensation through his insides.

He smiled. "I didn't wake up dead if that's what you're worried about."

"Oh, you!" She huffed and drew her hands back. Her gaze narrowed then widened. "It can't be! We can see each other!"

"Let there be light," he said, forcing his cramped muscles to bring him to his feet. He held out his hand to help her up.

She took it and rose beside him. "We need to find out where this wonderful illumination is coming from."

He gestured toward the passage they had yet to explore. "Seems to be beaming in from somewhere that way."

They entered the passage and soon encountered a breeze with an outdoorsy tang. Lauren let out a laugh that seemed more than a little giddy. Kent squeezed her hand that he had retained in his possession.

Shortly, the passage began to rise and narrow. They could no longer walk side-by-side, and Kent went ahead. The breeze grew fresher and the light stronger. Abruptly, he stepped out the side of the mountain onto a knoll looking down on a forest clearing. He stopped so suddenly that Lauren ran into him.

"Unbelievable!" The word gasped out of him.

"What?" Lauren pushed at him.

He stepped out of her way. She came up beside him and clamped both hands over her mouth, blinking rapidly.

Kent laid a hand on her shoulder. "Wait here inside the cave entrance. I need to investigate. People don't leave one of those things lying around unattended, and the attendant may not be friendly."

She nodded, tears shimmering in her eyes. Hope and fear struggled in the wobbly smile she sent his way.

Kent squared his shoulders and marched down the hill. With no cover available, there was no point in trying a subtle approach toward the last object he expected to see on the backside of nowhere—a Bell helicopter.

The bird was painted blue and white, and lacked identification markers on the chopper's body that would be present if it belonged to the US Forest Service, some other government agency or a business corporation. A private aircraft sitting here at the exit from the cave? Too convenient a coincidence to believe this mode of transportation wasn't connected with the scheme that involved the sabotage of his plane.

The nearer he drew toward the chopper the slower he approached, gaze searching for threat. No one appeared to be sitting inside the cockpit, but that didn't mean no one was there. A blue jay fluttered by a few feet from him, and he jumped, then shook himself and proceeded. The grass was thick and soft here, unlike the patchy growth in the scree around Trouble Creek. If anyone were snoozing inside the body of the aircraft, they wouldn't hear him coming. And they wouldn't see him either, because there were no passenger windows. This was a cargo chopper.

Kent reached the bird and peered through the cockpit window. No one in evidence.

Here goes nothing!

He grabbed the door handle, jerked it open and leaped into the pilot seat. No startled outcry greeted his plunging entrance, and he stuck his head into the cargo area. Empty, except for one telltale object—a long, narrow cart, ideal for hauling long, narrow, heavy crates through cave passages. The only serious obstacle would be the drop-off Lauren had fallen down, but the mastermind behind all this no doubt had a plan to deal with that minor hiccup. A wooden ramp would do it.

The mystery just became less mysterious. This was the escape vehicle for whoever had wrecked his plane, along with his loot of gold bars. No doubt Mags had been the intended pilot for this whirlybird, but now... Kent's brow furrowed then smoothed. Now *he* was the only pilot left in the game. No wonder the man mountain hadn't gutted him with the knife when he had the chance. Kent was still useful. Everyone else was throwaway baggage.

Kent turned to motion Lauren over, but she was already halfway across the clearing. She stopped beside the open pilot door and gazed up at him. He shared his deductions with her, and her lips flattened into a thin line as she nodded in agreement.

Her brow furrowed. "Can you summon help with this thing?"

"If we're not still disrupted by iron ore deposits," he said, plucking a battery-operated aviation radio unit from a slot in the center console between the front bucket seats. He switched on the radio and received a burst of static. The unit worked, but would it reach out to anyone?

Swallowing his stomach into place, Kent tuned to the emergency frequency then relayed the standard distress message once... twice...three times. No response except more white noise. His hopes fell as Lauren's shoulders slumped.

Static suddenly burst from the radio. A muffled voice came through, but no intelligible words.

Kent's heart leaped. He keyed the mic. "Say again?"

"Dyer Airport, Dyer, Nevada, US Bureau of Land Management, responding to distress call." Static still ruled, but the words were relatively clear. How long that would last was anybody's guess.

Kent spoke quickly but clearly, informing the technician about the crash landing of his airplane and the location in the abandoned mining town of Trouble Creek, Nevada, exact coordinates unavailable due to instrumentation failure prior to the crash. Garbled words responded briefly and then devolved into total static. Had the technician heard what he said?

A groan of wordless frustration came from Lauren. "Why are you using the battery-operated? Why not the built-in radio?"

Kent's gaze met the desperation in Lauren's. "We've got to get this bird in the air. It's the only way we'll send a clear message on either the battery or the built-in. There's one big obstacle." He frowned at the front instrument panel. "No key in the ignition."

THIRTEEN

The bottom dropped out of Lauren's stomach. "Here sits this beautiful helicopter, and we can't fly it?"

"I didn't say that." Kent grinned down at her from his perch in the pilot's seat. "I just said the missing key was an obstacle. I'm pretty sure I can hot-wire this baby."

"Kent Garland, don't scare me like that. I could just shake you."

"Hold that thought while you climb in on the other side of me."

"You want me to hold on to being angry with you?"

His gaze warmed. "You're especially beautiful when you're mad."

Lauren turned on her heel and stomped around the large helicopter. The guy was certifiable if he thought that sort of backhanded compliment was going to get on her good side.

Yet, a frisson of warmth flowed through her, and she swallowed a smile.

Then a thought chilled her blood.

What might be happening among the survivors back at the mercantile? Was her mother safe? The answer had to be a big "no." The saboteur was deadly dangerous. When Kent and his gun had not returned last night, the killer might have decided to take that opportunity to eliminate all the witnesses to his treachery. Who knew what horror could be happening this very minute on the other side of the mountain?

"Hurry!" Lauren cried as she climbed into the copilot seat.

Kent had stepped out of the chopper so he could lean in under the dash and fiddle with wires. All she could see of him was the back of his head and neck.

A sudden burst from the engine sent a jolt of electricity through Lauren, but then the purr died. Kent muttered something under his breath. Lauren clasped her hands together. *Please, God, help us get this helicopter airborne!* She held her breath as several heartbeats passed. The engine roared to healthy life, and Lauren let out an involuntary cheer.

Kent grinned at her as he hoisted himself

back into the pilot's seat. "Get your helmet on." He pointed to an object strapped to the roof of the chopper. Lauren complied, and Kent donned his also.

Her foot beat a ragged tattoo on the floor as she watched him run through a series of flight checks, flipping switches and pushing buttons on the front, middle and overhead consoles. She had no clue what he was doing, but lectured herself that all the fussy business must be necessary. Her stomach clenched. Something in her core knew beyond certainty that time was running out for the people trapped in Trouble Creek.

"Can you hear me?" Kent's voice came through the ear phones built into the helmet.

"Loud and clear," she answered. "Can we please—"

"Hang in there. I'm working as fast as I can."

"I know. I know. I just…sorry." Lauren gritted her teeth against pointless nagging.

Finally, the rotors began to turn—slowly at first, but then faster and faster until they were a blur. The helicopter lifted off the ground, and Lauren expelled a pent-up breath. They rose above the pine trees, and Kent turned the nose of the helicopter away from Trouble Creek.

"What are you doing?" she burst out. "We have to get back to the others as quickly as possible."

He shot her a glance. "Priority one is re-sending our distress call. And, if possible, I'd like to keep the people in Trouble Creek from hearing the noise of the chopper while we wait for the cavalry."

"I don't know how long we can wait, Kent. I have a very bad feeling. Our disappearance overnight may signal the saboteur that his greatest deterrent—you and your gun—has been removed."

"News flash, sweetheart. I don't have my gun."

"The saboteur doesn't know that."

Their gazes locked for a long second.

Kent shook his head and shrugged. "Let's get this Mayday sent. Then we'll see."

He brought them to a hover just beyond the next mountain. The scenery was breathtaking with snowy peaks, majestic rock faces and strips of brilliant green pines, but Lauren could appreciate none of it. With a reassuring nod, Kent flipped the switch to include her headset in the conversation on the built-in radio and made the call.

Thankfully, communication was now crystal clear. Unfortunately, the tiny Dyer airport—the nearest to their location—had no police or military helicopters on site. They were passed on to the local authorities in Las Vegas and were bumped up almost immediately to the field office of the FBI. Kent efficiently explained the situation to the special agent at the other end, and they were again immediately sent up the chain of authority.

Lauren exchanged a puzzled glance with Kent. A person would think emergency response could be activated without this crazy game of hot potato.

"Assistant Special Agent in Charge Rolanda Romero," said a crisp female voice. "Do I understand correctly that your plane was brought down by an onboard explosive device?"

"That's correct," Kent said. "We crash-landed in a valley in the Rockies near an abandoned mining town called Trouble Creek. Landslides have cut off ground access to the valley. We need air evacuation."

"As soon as possible," Lauren inserted. "We have injured people, as well as one fatality."

"Emergency services are prepping for departure as we speak," the ASAC said. "Can you tell me who was aboard the sabotaged aircraft?"

Kent named off those on the passenger list and then added himself and Magdalena

Haven. "Ms. Haven is the fatality, but we have reason to think she was a party to the sabotage. We believe that she and a confederate among the passengers intended to debark by parachute prior to the explosion. Either the bomb went off prematurely, or they were behind on their departure. The tandem chute was never used."

"Do you know the identity of Ms. Haven's confederate?"

"We do not, but covert attempts have been made to kill off the survivors. You are advised to send law enforcement along with emergency services."

"Noted. Our copy of the flight manifest lists Marlin Barrington among the passengers. Are you certain he is not with you?"

"Positive." Lauren rolled her eyes. "He's my stepfather. My mother was on board, but her husband was not."

"We know who you are…and your mother."

Something in the ASAC's tone curdled Lauren's insides. "Why do you want to know about Marlin?"

"He disappeared the day your plane took off. The same day we were closing the net to arrest him for massive fraud and insider trading, among a laundry list of other crimes."

Lauren's heart plummeted to her toes. "My poor mom. She'll be devastated."

Kent reached over and squeezed her hand. Lauren shot him a grateful look.

"We will be speaking to her and to you," said Romero.

"Wait just a minute. If you think my mother or I had anything to do with—"

"Something you should know for your own safety," the ASAC interrupted. "Barrington is not this man's real name. He has had many aliases over the course of several decades of criminal activity."

Kent cleared his throat. "Would that criminal activity include the heist of buffalo-head gold coins?"

Stone silence answered.

"What do you know about that robbery?" Romero spoke at last.

"In one of the caves, I came across such a coin, as well as a small furnace and bar molds. We were in an emergency situation at that moment, so I didn't have time to check out the crates in the cavern, but I wouldn't be surprised if they hold gold bars."

"We will be there within three hours." The ASAC spoke briskly. "Do whatever you can to stay safe until we arrive."

"Roger that," Kent said. "Since you were on

Barrington's trail, you must have been watching for our flight to land in San Francisco."

"That is correct. We were going to arrest him as soon as he stepped off the plane."

"So while you were keeping an eye on us," Lauren inserted, "he hightailed it in a different direction."

"Not necessarily. Had matters gone as planned by the saboteurs, eventually we would have found the wreckage, and it would not have been out of the ordinary for little or nothing to remain of the bodies after critters had done their scavenging."

Lauren shuddered.

"We would have been forced to conclude Barrington died in the crash," Romero went on, "along with the rest of you. That way, he could disappear, and no one would be looking for him. But since the plan with the parachute was disrupted, it is probable he's with you among the survivors."

"I know what my stepfather looks like," Lauren snapped. "He's not here!"

"You know only the face that he showed you. This man is a chameleon. He's on the FBI and Interpol's most wanted lists, but we have no picture of his true appearance because no one knows what he really looks like."

Kent let out a whistle. "Let me ask you

this. Is there a name on the passenger manifest filed with the ground crew that is different than the on-board list I named off?"

The ASAC let out a thoughtful hum. "Yes, there is."

Lauren held her breath. Who would it be? Cliff? Dirk? Phil?

"Neil Gleason," Romero pronounced. "We'll run that name through the system, but I'm pretty sure we'll find out he doesn't exist."

Lauren's jaw dropped. That endearing old curmudgeon? She'd seen nothing of the Marlin she knew in the grandfatherly persona. Even her mother hadn't recognized him. And yet, now that she'd been told who he was, it made sense why he wouldn't allow her to examine him too closely after the crash.

While Kent ended the radio communication with ASAC Romero, Lauren's mind traveled a mile a minute, peeling back the disguise.

The slight slur in his speech wasn't because of dentures, but from false teeth that created an altered facial profile. Glasses masked his eyes. But those eyes were brown, and Marlin's had been blue. Gleason was not wearing contacts to change the eye color—she knew because she'd shined her penlight into them— but the Marlin persona might have worn them. Such a clever and detailed disguise, even to the age spots on his hands. Not difficult to fake with a little pigment injected under the skin. Dying and cutting his hair differently was also a simple no-brainer.

Neil's height was different than Marlin's, but extra padding in the shoes could alter that; Marlin was lean as a whip, but again, padding for Neil was a simple solution. When she'd landed on top of him during the air crisis, she'd noticed the softness of his middle, but it hadn't occurred to her it was fake. The scruffy beard he'd been growing since the crash had only added to the camouflage.

Nausea cramped Lauren's insides. How was she ever going to break this news to her mother? Hadn't Mom been through enough with Lauren's father? Now, mom's new chance at love was proving as hollow as the first— maybe more so. At least her first husband hadn't been a crook, just a boy who refused to grow up.

For the first time, pity rather than resentment washed through Lauren for the man who had missed her childhood. His loss as much as hers. Whatever fears drove him to run from responsibility also cost him his dignity and self-respect. What was the chance he was happy wherever he was today? Not much. Cowardice was a cancer. It was past time for

Lauren to let him go if ever she wanted to stop robbing herself of enjoying a true relationship by refusing to trust.

A tiny flower of hope unfurled in her heart. The excellent man by her side said he wanted to be with her! How could she reject such a precious blessing? Sure, she'd take things slowly—let them both prove their feelings were as real in the calm times as they were in the storm. Let herself grow into the idea of permanence. She was ready to stop holding this man at arm's length. Ready to finally take that risk with her heart.

A small laugh left her throat. Kent shot her a questioning look.

"It's nothing," she said. "And it's everything. I think I just saw myself clearly for the first time in a long time. It's daunting and liberating all at once."

He offered a lift of the eyebrows. "Sounds intriguing, but we'll have to pursue this topic later. Look." He waved toward the darkening sky. "Storm coming. A big one. Barometer's dropping like crazy. We have to put this bird down and take cover in the cave."

Lauren shook her head. "We have to go to Trouble Creek. Marlin… Neil…whoever…is a desperate man. We can't trust him with my mom or the others."

"Sure, but *you'll* be in danger if we go back there. That's not okay with me. Help is on the way. Let's let the professionals handle this."

"Law enforcement and emergency services are at least three hours out, and this storm is likely to delay them. We can't wait! I'll never forgive myself if something happens to my mother that I could have prevented."

Lauren held her unwavering stare on Kent. His jaw muscles flexed, and he made busy work of holding the helicopter steady as they bounced with increasing frequency in the strengthening turbulence.

At last, he jerked a nod. "If it was my mom I'd feel the same way, but I don't have to like it."

Kent's gut churned as he eased the helicopter toward the ground at the edge of Trouble Creek. The people in the mercantile would have heard their approach a long time ago, and yet no one had run outside to greet them. There should be jubilation by now. Were they being held hostage...or worse? A keening noise from Lauren telegraphed her distress.

The chopper landed with a minor bump. He shut down the rotors and disconnected the hotwires, killing the engine.

"I'm going in the front door," he told Lauren.

"You come in the back and lurk in the storage room until we figure out what's going on."

"I need to make sure Mom is safe."

"Understood. But we have to do what we can to avoid making a bad situation worse. If it turns out that Neil is on the rampage, and he has a weapon of some sort, get out quick and go into hiding. He may not know you're with me. He'll probably think the man mountain got you. Stay safe until help arrives."

Lauren's jaw jutted, and those jade eyes went hard as stone. "Not happening. I'm going to be right there, giving you what backup I can. Even if it's only to serve as a distraction. We're in this together all the way."

Kent fought the urge to bang his head on the dashboard. Talk about stubborn! But brave, too, and he had to give her credit for the ultimate loyalty when it came to loved ones. Would he ever be counted among those? They'd have to survive the next few hours in order to create that opportunity.

"All right then," he said. "We'll have to wing it. We don't know what situation we'll be walking into. Keep a cool head. No heroics."

She offered a grim smile. "No more than yours."

He'd have to be satisfied with that much assurance, which was basically none.

Kent removed his helmet, Lauren did the same, and they hopped out of the chopper in tandem. Dust devils kissed his face from the slowing rotors and increasing wind. The sky had darkened to ominous pewter pocked with roiling dark clouds. The temperature wasn't cold enough for snow, but almost. They were soon in for a bone-chilling rain.

He trotted around the helicopter and joined Lauren in the sheltering lee of the decrepit livery stable. Her shadowed gaze met his. He cupped her chin in one hand, allowing his thumb to trace the path of her elegantly arched cheek bone.

"Let's survive this. Okay?"

Her hand covered his. "Okay."

Tearing himself away from the warmth of her touch, he motioned for her to head for the back of the main buildings. He watched her take off with a lithe stride that belied the nerves that must be tearing her up inside. Sorely missing the weight of his Beretta, Kent made himself turn and head for the mercantile.

Along the route, he picked up a loose two-by-four with a couple of rusty nails sticking out. If Neil/Marlin got within clobbering distance, he wasn't going to hesitate.

Softly climbing the wooden steps to the

mercantile, he listened for any noise from inside. Only the whistle of the wind answered him. As he approached the door, a porch board squeaked beneath his feet. He winced, but the telltale sound was unavoidable. Most of the old boards squeaked.

Too bad they'd blocked up every window in the place. He couldn't even take a preliminary peek at what lay within.

Where was Lauren? Had she reached the rear entrance of the mercantile?

No point in delaying the inevitable. Kent pressed his back against the wall to the side of the door, turned the doorknob with one hand and thrust it open. At first there was no sound to indicate there was a living being within. Then a soft, slimy chuckle raised the hairs on the back of his neck.

"Come on in, Kent. Just as well you found the helicopter. We'll be leaving now."

Squaring his shoulders and hefting the board, Kent stepped into the mercantile. His gaze scanned the dim interior in the light of a single kerosene lantern. He released a pent-up breath.

At least he wasn't viewing bloody carnage. All the arbitrage executives were seated on the floor in front of the potbellied stove, gagged and bound together with leather straps. Kent's gaze fixed on a sneering Neil/Marlin standing nearby. One of his hands squeezed the arm of a white-faced Nina, and the other hand pointed Kent's Beretta at her head.

"How did you get my gun?"

"Rolly gave it to me after he captured you."

"I assume you're referring to the Neanderthal of the mountain. How did you connect with him without being seen?"

"We had a stash spot agreed upon where we could pass notes or items to one another. It's not that hard to disappear for a few minutes. Now, what have you done with my cousin?"

"He was your cousin?"

"Was? Oh, dear! That's too bad. I'm not terribly surprised you outsmarted him, though. He was never the sharpest tool in the shed, and his back-to-nature lifestyle was abhorrent, but he served his purposes. At least, he finished turning the coins into bars before he met his end at your hands."

Kent clamped his lips together. Neil wasn't going to hear it from him that it was Lauren who had bested dear old Rolly. Maybe Neil would assume the matter turned out the other way around, and she was no longer a factor.

"Nina, dear," Neil said, "kindly tell your daughter to come out of the storage area."

Kent's heart fell. So much for the hope of keeping Lauren's presence a secret.

"Do it!" Neil shook his wife, and she let out a sharp whimper.

"No need to get rough," Lauren clipped out as she entered the front room.

Nina moaned. "Oh, sweetheart, I'm so sorry. I fell for the wrong man again."

"He told you who he is under the disguise?"

Nina shook her head. "He didn't have to tell me. That mannerism of scrubbing his chin with his hand like Marlin used to do. It took me a while, but this morning I suddenly *saw.* I planned to pretend like I was still in the dark and clobber him with the shovel when his back was turned, but I'm not good at deception. He took one look at my face and knew I knew. That's when he pulled a gun."

Neil/Marlin smirked. "Nina, honey, you always were too wholesome and transparent. That's what made you the perfect cover wife—charming, attractive, age-appropriate, generous with my stolen money. You even made sure I showed up in church every Sunday." He laughed. "With you on my arm, I looked squeaky clean."

She glared up at her scoundrel of a husband. "Not to God, you didn't. You should really worry about that."

"Enough jabber!" Neil hauled his hostage with him back against the glass-fronted counter where a small pile of leather straps lay. His sharp gaze darted between Kent and Lauren. "You!" He nodded toward Kent. "Get rid of the board. And you." He nodded toward Lauren. "Come stand by my fellow investment brokers."

Kent tossed the board, and it landed with a sharp clatter. Lauren stepped over to the group of bound men where she'd been directed to go.

"I don't understand something," she said. "I get it that under your direction Rolly stuffed the pine boughs down our stovepipe and rigged up the other traps, but why did he burn down his own cabin?"

Kent hid a small grin at Lauren's stalling tactic. Keep the bad guy distracted and talking, and maybe an opportunity to overpower him might present itself.

Neil's mouth twisted like he'd sampled something sour. "That wasn't *his* cabin. It was mine. You didn't think I was going to stay in that disgusting cave, did you? The cabin was fitted out comfortably for when Mags and I arrived in camp to prepare my gold for transport. But then we *all* landed on his doorstep.

"Rolly resented the extra company. On the second night, that impatient fool put a magnifying glass in a box full of dry straw and set it on top of the cabin. That morning, I found a note in our stash spot warning me of what was going to happen to my cabin when the sun came out. As soon as our merry little group started climbing the cliffs to plant our glass shards, I hustled back toward town to stop it but I was too late. The idiot burned down the cabin to get back at me because I hadn't yet fulfilled my promise to deliver *you* to him." He leered at Lauren. A growl left Kent's throat, and Neil stabbed the gun barrel in his direction. "Down, boy. No time for that."

"Marlin, you are disgusting vermin." Nina's eyes spat fire.

He shoved her away from him. "You didn't think so when you said 'I do,' darling."

A pair of tears slid down Nina's cheeks, and Lauren took her mother in her arms.

"How touching." Neil's lips twisted in an ugly sneer. "Now, dear stepdaughter, please rope my *wife* in with the cozy group by the fire." He tossed the pile of leather straps onto the floor at her feet. "No more chitchat."

White-faced, Lauren complied. Soon, Nina was seated and bound with the others.

"Go stand by the flyboy," Neil ordered Lauren.

As she took her place by his side, Kent had

all he could do not to grab her and hold her close. She was quivering from head to toe. White heat spread through his chest. If only he could bury his fist in this creep's nose.

Holding his gun and his gaze steady on Kent and Lauren, Neil bent and tested the bindings. "Good enough." He nodded.

"What now?" Kent glared at Neil.

The older man showed his teeth in a savage grin. "And now, we're going to get out of Dodge."

"We can't. It's too dangerous. There's a bad storm bearing down on us."

"We'll take our chances. I have no doubt you've notified the feds of our location. Your actions force me to leave without my gold, and for that you will pay." His gaze narrowed into venomous slits. "However, from my other enterprises, I have more than sufficient resources stashed away to be comfortable for the next eternity. I'm not sticking around for the gunfight at the OK Corral."

Kent's skin tightened. Neil's reference to the famous Old-West shoot-out exposed desperate resolve not to be captured by law enforcement. This guy would gun down anyone in his path and take crazy chances with his life in order to stay free. The only person he wouldn't shoot was his pilot—at least until he was in the clear. Maybe Kent could work that slender thread of immunity in his favor.

He lifted his hands in a show of surrender. "We'd better get going then."

"Not so fast." Neil motioned for Lauren to precede him. "I think I'll gain more cooperation if your girlfriend accompanies us."

"Girlfriend?" Kent lifted his eyebrows. "What gave you that idea?"

Was his desperate disclaimer hurtful to Lauren? She kept her head down so he had no idea.

Neil rolled his eyes. "Oh, please, you two have been a couple of flints knocking sparks off each other ever since we were dumped here. Only a matter of time until a fire starts."

Lauren's head jerked up. "That's nonsense!"

Kent frowned. Did he dare hope her vehement objection was as disingenuous as his? No time to worry about that. "Look. You don't have to—"

"No argument. Get moving." He herded them toward the door.

"Never forget, I love you, Lauren!" Nina called after them.

"I love you, too, Mom!" Lauren answered in choked tones.

Neil responded by shoving her into Kent and forcing them to head outside. The rising wind whipped strands of Lauren's ponytail around her pale cheeks. She fixed a terrified gaze on Kent's face. He offered the slightest shake of his head. Their make-or-break moment hadn't come yet. At least the others would get to wait for rescue in shelter and safety.

As their captor followed them outside, he suddenly whirled and fired a shot into the building. Glass shattered. Lauren let out a cry and stampeded toward the mercantile. Kent grabbed for her but Neil caught her on the first step and shoved the barrel of his gun into her temple. She froze with a whimper, and Kent's hands fisted. He held himself in check. Barely.

"Relax," Neil said. "I didn't shoot anybody. Let's go!"

He hurried them up the street with more barked orders and shoving. The wind was kicking up a dust storm. A few large drops of icy rain splatted onto Kent's head—just the beginning of what this storm was about to do. He hadn't exaggerated the danger of taking off in this.

They reached the chopper, and Neil dug a key out of his pocket. "Get this thing going," he said with a smirk, handing it to Kent.

Seething rebellion concealed beneath slumped shoulders, Kent took the key. He climbed into the bird, jammed his helmet onto his head and began pre-flight procedure. A rumble behind him signaled the opening of the cargo door. Neil and his gun climbed into the open cargo area, leaving Lauren hugging herself in the rain.

"Get in very slowly and carefully," their captor told her. "And you," he nodded toward Kent, "stick to business. I'll shoot her dead and wound you if you try anything."

Kent abandoned the pre-flight checklist. Normal procedure wasn't going to matter anyway. As Lauren climbed inside, he started the rotors.

"Shut that door and let's get going," Neil snapped.

"What about our helmets?" Lauren protested. "Shouldn't we put those on?"

Kent hid a grin. Good girl. She was subtly digging in her heels with that stalling tactic again. He ramped up the rotor speed.

"Give me a break!" their captor snarled. "I've got a loaded gun pointed in your direction, and you're worried about a helmet? Shut the door. You're letting the rain in."

Kent watched out of the corner of his eye as Lauren slowly turned and reached for the door handle.

Now!

At his abrupt jerk on the controls, the chopper leaped from the earth. He yanked the stick sideways, and Lauren tumbled out of the aircraft with a high-pitched yelp. Kent hauled the stick back, sending the bird into a steep climb even as a sharp report from the Beretta deafened his ears.

Sudden pain seared through Kent's shoulder as he struggled for control of the wildly bucking helicopter. The world spun in crazy circles, and blackness fought to claim him.

FOURTEEN

Lauren sprawled facedown in the muck, gasping for breath. Sharp fingernails of ice stabbed her shivering body. What? Who? Oh, that was only the rain. Her mind scrambled to make sense of what had just happened.

Kent had dumped her out of the chopper at the same instant as he took off! Where was he?

She scrambled to her feet, gazing upward, oblivious to the raindrops that pelted her eyeballs. There! About a flagpole's height above the earth, the helicopter dipped and slewed crazily in the murky sky. The thunder of the rotors blended with the roar of the storm. Her fist went to her mouth as the aircraft went into a spin. She bit down as it plunged to the ground and lay churning on its side.

Without a second thought, Lauren raced toward the crash site. The rotors screamed as they fought earth's iron grip. One broke off and flew into the murk. Another snapped, and Lauren ducked as it whipped past her. The remaining two gave up in a gasp of smoke as the motor burned out.

Crying Kent's name, she reached the helicopter and yanked the pilot's door open. He dangled in his seat belt, helmeted head slumped, dark blood soaking his shoulder. Kent groaned. *Thank you, God!* He was alive.

She unzipped his bomber jacket and ripped aside the layered shirts under it to expose his left shoulder. A through-and-through bullet wound near the clavicle spat a narrow trickle of blood, not a gushing stream. So far, so good. The bullet appeared to have missed the major arteries in this area of the body, though she couldn't rule out internal bleeding. She unsnapped his helmet, tossed it to the side and examined his mouth and nose. No sign of bloody froth, which indicated that the bullet had also missed the lung. Emergency intervention could be delayed until they reached shelter.

"I'm going to get you out of here," she murmured as she worked at the stubborn seat belt from her awkward access to the tilted helicopter. "Don't you worry about a thing. I'm here to take care of you."

Kent groaned and lifted his head. Bleary gray eyes blinked at her.

"We've got to get you back to the mercantile and my first-aid kit," she told him.

"Neil?" he croaked.

"I don't care about him as long as he's not shooting at us."

Lauren pulled herself up on the tilted landing gear to peer deeper into the aircraft. The murderous crook's body lay limp across the wheeled cart in the cargo bay. His right arm was twisted at an awkward angle. The Beretta was nowhere in evidence.

She sniffed. "If he's alive, he won't be firing a gun anytime soon."

Kent let out a pained chuckle. "This is the first time I've glimpsed the ruthless side of Lauren. Remind me not to get too carried away antagonizing you."

"That part of me is reserved for dirty thugs who try to kill my mom and the man I—well, the man I think I—love." There, she'd said it. Terrifying, exhilarating words.

"Love? I like that." Kent's grin was loopy as she helped him half climb, half fall out of the helicopter into the freezing rain.

"Don't go all delusional now." She slung his good arm over her shoulders. "By the time we get you back to town, you won't remember a thing I said."

"I'll remember."

Together, they made slow but steady progress. Kent seemed to be doing his best, putting one foot in front of the other, but he was no lightweight and leaned heavily on her for support. For one of the few times in her life, Lauren gave thanks for her sturdy athlete's body, rather than the dainty build a lot of men seemed to prefer.

They reached the livery stable and halted for a breather. Kent took his arm from around her and propped himself against the side of the building, eyes closed. Lauren took another look at his wound. No change, but he was definitely white around the lips and could be going into shock, especially with the freezing wet to contend with.

"I think we need to get you inside the stable," she told him. "I'll run to the mercantile, free the other folks, and get Cliff to help me bring the transport wagon back with blankets and my kit."

It was a testimony to the level of Kent's pain that he nodded his head. Suddenly, he straightened and stared into the storm in the direction of the mercantile that was barely visible through the driving rain.

"Smoke," he said through gritted teeth.

Lauren turned her head away from the rain and sniffed the air. "Smoke!" she echoed. Way more of it than could possibly be coming from the stove chimney.

The gun blast and sound of breaking glass as they left the mercantile played through her memory. Chills coursed up her spine. That vile monster had shot the kerosene lamp! Those old planks would go up like a torch. Even with the pouring rain outside, by now every last person in the mercantile could have burned alive or perished from smoke inhalation.

Lauren broke from Kent at a dead run. Visions of Rolly's last flaming moments tortured her mind. Not her mother! Not those other innocent people! Even Dirk didn't deserve to go that way!

She splashed to a halt in front of the mercantile. Tongues of fire shot out the roof of the building, hissing and spitting at the waves of falling water that fought to drown it.

"Motherrrr!" she shrieked and headed for the door.

A strong arm snaked around her and clasped her to a solid body. "It's too late," Kent's voice spoke in her ear. "There's nothing we can do."

With an eerie howl like a dying thing, the

roof collapsed, and the building became a smoldering wreck. Here and there tongues of fire sought to defy the rain, but it was a losing battle. Lauren's knees buckled, and she hit the mud, overwhelmed with wrenching sobs.

"Laurennn!" Someone materialized from the murky weather, walking toward them.

"Mom?"

"Nina?"

Lauren's amazed identification mingled with Kent's.

"Oh, my darling daughter!" Her mother knelt and gathered Lauren into her arms. "I thought I'd lost you."

Weeping into her mother's sodden shoulder, Lauren shook her head. "I thought I'd lost *you!*"

"We're all in the transport wagon."

Lauren lifted her head. "But how did you escape the mercantile?"

"Let's get out of the rain before explanation time."

Lauren heaved to her feet, casting her eyes around for Kent. She found him sprawled on his back in the mud, unmoving. Her stomach clenched as the medical truth seized her.

Oh, God, You wouldn't be so cruel, would You? Finally, she'd discovered a man she could trust with her heart, and now this.

Between hypothermia and shock, if the cavalry didn't arrive very soon, Trouble Creek might yet see another death.

Kent struggled to consciousness in fits and starts, as if he were climbing on his hands and knees up a mountain of mud that stood between him and the sunlight. Gradually, laboriously, he'd near the peak, the light on the other side so close he could feel it. Voices—some familiar, some not—would tease his ears, and then he'd slide down again into deep darkness and silence.

At last he surged over the top of the mud mountain and arrived at a single, stunning awareness. He was *not* cold. In fact, he was toasty warm and cushioned on a soft, accommodating mattress. Not all was comfort, though. Heat throbbed in his shoulder, and a mild headache danced around his consciousness like a yappy, little dog, more annoyance than attention-grabber.

His eyelids parted, and he squinted up at a beautiful sight. Seated by his bed, Lauren smiled down at him. Her hair was loose, softly framing her face in an auburn cloud. The pale, gaunt quality of her skin had given way to the healthy glow of someone who was warm, hydrated and well-fed.

"How are you feeling, big guy?" Concern clouded those vivid jade eyes as both her hands squeezed one of his.

"Hungry." A low growl from his stomach underscored his raspy word. "And thirsty."

Lauren laughed, a glorious sound. "I think I can do something about the thirsty part."

She retrieved a lidded container and put a straw to his lips. Cool, fresh water bathed his parched tongue and throat.

"Where are we?" The words came out a little less rough.

"Summerlin Hospital in Las Vegas. We've been here for nearly thirty-six hours. You were shot, remember?"

"It's a memory I could do without, but the icy rain was worse." He shuddered, sending a twinge through his shoulder.

"I was terrified I was going to lose you." A shadow crossed her face. "By the time the emergency rescue team arrived, your body temperature had fallen dangerously low. If not for that ratty old leather bomber jacket that kept your torso relatively dry, I don't know if you would have made it. Not with the blood loss and trauma from your wound on top of hypothermia."

"I don't suppose you saved that ratty old jacket. I'm sort of fond of it."

"That old thing? It had through-and-through bullet holes in it and the lining was soaked in blood. What do you think?"

Kent looked away and heaved out a breath. He'd get over the loss—eventually. A giggle from Lauren brought his head around.

He narrowed his eyes. "I take it you're teasing me?" He'd intended to sound fierce, but the question came out pitifully hopeful.

She tweaked his nose and grinned. "You can thank my mother. She explained to me about men's old, comfortable clothing. We're having it dry-cleaned and refurbished. Frankly, I'd be willing to bronze the thing and mount it on a pedestal for saving your life."

His face eased into an answering grin. "I'm pretty sure you had something to do with keeping me among the living."

"I wish I could have done more, but I didn't have much to work with. When we got to the hospital, you needed a bit of surgical repair on your scapula and rotator cuff, but the doc says with therapy you'll completely recover. The medical staff took great care of you—well, all of us—and here we are, safe and sound."

"Everyone?"

Lauren's upper lip curled back. "All but the bad guys." She paused with a frown. "No, actually, Neil aka Marlin aka aliases-into-infinity is still with us, but he's in bad shape. They think he'll pull through, but his spine was injured in the helicopter crash. It's almost certain he'll never walk again." Her gaze darkened. "To be honest, I sometimes struggle with the urge to storm past the federal agents guarding his hospital room and throttle him, but then I remind myself that spending the rest of his life behind bars in a wheelchair is probably perfect justice for the misery he's caused to so many—my mother not least of all."

Kent squeezed her hand. "How is Nina doing?"

"Not so good emotionally. Physically she's fine, and she's definitely the heroine of the hour with the arbitrage executives."

"The fire!"

Lauren nodded. "Remember that board full of nails you threw on the floor? She snagged it with her feet and punctured off her bonds with one of the nails. Then she helped the others get loose, and they all helped each other get out of the mercantile before the fire overcame them."

"She *is* a heroine."

"Not in her own eyes. She's still beating herself up for marrying a charming crook who makes Al Capone look like an upstanding citizen. I've had a few chats with Assistant Special Agent in Charge Rolanda Romero. She's shed light on a few things, but not overmuch. The feds can be pretty tight-lipped."

Kent grimaced. "Not sure I really want the gory details, but go on."

Lauren looked away and pursed her lips, as if she was gathering herself for a distasteful task. "Okay, here goes. The mountain man we encountered has a rap sheet a mile long. No big surprise, but now that the FBI has linked Marlin Barrington to his cousin Roland Cullen, they've figured out Marlin started life as Raymond Cullen. Rolly and Ray spent their formative years in neighboring tumbledown trailers in the foothills of the Rocky Mountains. No fathers in the picture. Bitter, abusive mothers. Eventually, they both wound up in the foster care system. Rolly grew up to become a thug, everything from a leg-breaker for loan sharks to petty drug dealer, but he had a smart aleck mouth and made one of the big-league players angry. The guy relieved Rolly of his tongue. After that, Rolly retreated from society to the mountaineer lifestyle he knew well.

"Ray, on the other hand, due to near genius intellect, came steadily up in the world. He planned and carried out heists and cons with ever greater proficiency and profits. But there was always a lot of angry thug in him, too. Plenty of dead bodies along the trail. The authorities would close in, and he'd disappear and start in somewhere else as someone else. At some point, he learned to fit in with the rich and famous, invented his own pedigree and proceeded to scam in the millions, not mere thousands. Some of the best and brightest in the so-called 'upper crust' fell prey to his charismatic genius for con games."

Kent let out a low whistle. "Then your mom is in good company. She shouldn't feel so much the fool."

Lauren wrinkled her nose. "The thing is, in his Marlin persona, he was genuinely good to my mother—until he decided killing her was in his best interest. Apparently, he didn't want to leave anyone behind who could potentially have a clue about where he might be hiding if the feds didn't buy his faked death in the airplane crash. Mom might be too trusting where charming men are concerned, but she's intelligent and observant. Too dangerous to just dump and run."

Heat coiled in Kent's middle. "He must have thought the same about you."

Lauren shrugged one shoulder. "He knew I held him in no esteem. His ego was insulted. Offing me was gravy."

"And the other passengers were collateral damage?"

"Richard Engle, yes. He's completely innocent. And, by the way, his knee has been surgically repaired, and he should recover fully. Cliff is in the clear, too, even though he worked for Peerless One. He's a Christian man with solid morals. But for Dirk and Phil there's good news and bad news. Marlin needed to eliminate them because they were in on the stock fraud scheme with him. He's not one to leave witnesses behind."

"So they survived but they're going to prison?"

"For a little while. That's the good news part. Since they've agreed to testify against Marlin—nail him but good in court—they'll receive lighter sentences."

"I guess you never know about people. Phil was such a trouper under dire conditions."

"I think he surprised himself. Found new depths he didn't know he had. I've visited him, and he apologized for his part in the arbitrage scam that led to Marlin's decision to sabotage your plane. He has his tale of woe and desperation as to why he got involved in something illegal at the office."

Kent's heart squeezed, and he turned his gaze toward the stark white wall.

"You're thinking about Mags?" Lauren's question was asked gently, but it cut like a knife.

He nodded. "She had her own tale of woe and desperation. Bitter divorce, nasty car accident, chronic pain, addiction to prescription drugs, but to agree to kill us all…" His voice faded away. "It makes you question who you can trust."

Lauren cupped his cheek and gently turned his face toward her. "You've changed my thinking about trust and about faith. If we don't hang on to those things—especially trust and faith in God—any of us could wind up doing what these people have done."

Kent covered her hand with his. "You're a wise woman, you know that? Compassionate, brave and strong. I thank God we met."

Color unfurled across her cheeks. "Me, too. Are you game for thanking God for each other for a long time to come?"

"Try lifelong." He grinned.

She smiled back, jade eyes dancing. "We could work on that."

"But sometime in the near future, how about a juicy cheeseburger?"

Lauren shook her head and chuckled. "Toast and gelatin or applesauce to start with, mister."

Kent scowled. "Okay, but could I talk you into something more substantial first?"

Her eyebrows rose.

"I'm starving for a kiss."

"Anything for my hero pilot," she murmured as she leaned close.

The tenderness of her lips on his sank deeply into his heart. Yes, he understood he was signing on for an adorable, scheming mother-in-law. The sooner, the better, because then Lauren would be his wife.

EPILOGUE

Six Months Later

"I'm excited and terrified at the same time," Lauren told her mother, who was sitting across from her in Kent's new Challenger 350 charter jet.

His insurance had finally done the right thing and replaced his plane.

"I don't blame you for either emotion," Mom answered with a smile and a pat on Lauren's knee. "But I can't think of any two people more deserving."

Lauren wrinkled her nose. "You're a bit prejudiced."

Mom laughed. "Can't blame a mother for that."

Lauren inhaled a deep breath and let it out slowly as she allowed her attention to drift toward the window. Bright sunshine illuminated the beehive of traffic and the structures below that were Washington, DC. They were descending toward Dulles International Airport in preparation for landing.

"Everyone doing okay back there?"

Kent's strong, deep voice from the cockpit sent a thrill through Lauren.

"We're doing great," Mom answered. "Very smooth flight, as usual."

Lauren grinned. She and Kent had been a couple ever since the rescue, and her appreciation of him had done nothing but grow. He was the real deal—solid and dependable. Actually, in her opinion, he alone should receive the Presidential Citizens Medal, rather than sharing the spotlight with her this afternoon at the award ceremony.

Not that either of them cared about the recognition. It was just something that happened in this day and age when extraordinary events like what had taken place in Trouble Creek occurred.

The media storm had been a mind-bending ride. One that wasn't over yet, but it hadn't been entirely terrible. Public fascination with their ordeal and the capture of a wanted fugitive had given rise to a wide variety of news agencies and other communications companies courting them for interviews and book and movie deals. Unsettling to the quiet life they both preferred, but good things were happening as a result.

Lauren and Kent had engaged the services of a Christian agent to help them deal with the intense scrutiny—not in order to leverage the attention for personal gain, but to carefully and wisely manage their time and their choices for media exposure. So far, they had done a smattering of tastefully orchestrated interviews, signed a book deal with a publisher whose reputable ghostwriter would do fine things with the story and allowed a Christian-based production company to option the movie rights.

Whatever anyone else chose to believe about their much-touted courage, Lauren and Kent wanted the glory for their survival to go to God, not their human efforts. In addition, the profits from the book and the potential movie were set up to funnel into a foundation to help victims of white-collar crime get back on their feet. Too often these innocent people were suddenly left destitute and without hope of recouping even the smallest portion of what had been stolen from them.

Lauren turned her head and smiled at the freshly minted director of that foundation. She couldn't think of anyone more ideally suited in temperament and experience to oversee the operation of the charitable organization than her mother. The responsibility was already proving therapeutic for her.

In a few short minutes, Kent brought the plane into a smooth landing, and Lauren unbuckled her seat belt in preparation to exit.

"Hold it!" Kent's urgent tone froze her in place. "Hang on a minute."

He emerged from the cockpit and stepped toward her, looking smart and professional in his pilot's uniform of black slacks and white shirt, but his face was grim and pale.

Lauren's heart plummeted. "What's the matter?"

Mom swiveled toward him, eyebrows raised.

"Nothing." Kent stopped beside Lauren's seat and gazed down at her. Those gray depths still managed to make her feel swept away into the clouds. If only this moment didn't suggest a storm was coming from somewhere.

"Well, I *hope* nothing." He shifted from one foot to another, his gaze sliding away toward the roof of the plane.

"Kent Garland," Mom said, rising, "I've never seen you unsure of yourself. What on earth is going on?"

Color crept from beneath the collar of his shirt and up onto his chiseled cheekbones. "You're right." He looked at them. "I'm sorry.

I'm scaring you with my jitters, and that's the opposite of what I intend."

"What do you intend?" Lauren stood and met his gaze.

"I can't wait," he said. "I meant to hold off until tonight after the banquet, but I think I'll go nuts if I don't know your answer before we do all the pomp and circumstance."

"Shall I step outside while you talk to my daughter?" Mom asked.

Kent flickered a smile in her direction. "No, that's fine. You should be here for this."

Lauren frowned and shook her head. "Do you mind helping me escape the pins and needles with a little explanation?"

"Okay." He nodded. "Just don't laugh at me or think this is too corny, but I'm going to be old-fashioned."

He grabbed both of Lauren's hands in a firm grip and went down on one knee.

Mom gasped.

Lauren gaped.

Kent's gaze captured hers with sober intensity. "Lauren Carter, I love you more than my next breath. Would you do me the honor of becoming my wife at the earliest possible moment?"

Stunned, Lauren slid a glance toward her mother.

"This has to be your choice, dear," Mom said, hands spread, palms up.

A brilliant smile crept from Lauren's heart onto her face. "There is no choice. It's a done deal. I love you, Kent Garland, and I can hardly wait to be your wife."

A bass whoop left Kent's lips, and he lunged to his feet, pulling a small velvet-covered box from his pocket. A gold ring topped with the glitter of a large diamond in a cluster of smaller diamonds made its way onto the appropriate finger.

Before she could examine the precious symbol of forever, Lauren found herself crushed in a happy embrace, warm lips on hers. She gladly answered Kent's kiss, as sweet peace and total trust mingled with the excitement of the new chapter opening in her life. *Their* life…together.

* * * * *

*If you enjoyed this book, don't miss
these other exciting stories
from Jill Elizabeth Nelson:*

*EVIDENCE OF MURDER
WITNESS TO MURDER
CALCULATED REVENGE
LEGACY OF LIES
BETRAYAL ON THE BORDER
FRAME-UP
SHAKE DOWN*

*Find these and other great reads
at www.LoveInspired.com*

Dear Reader,

How deeply does it affect us when someone intimately close abandons us? Does such abandonment plant seeds of rejection and bitterness deep within our hearts? How could it not? Even many who have faith in God struggle with the tragic legacy of abandonment.

Broken families—fathers or mothers walking away from their responsibilities as parents—is an epidemic in our society. We need look no further than today's news, the neighbors down the street, or perhaps our own households to see the consequences in terms of unhappy lives, inability to trust in others or God, or even a myriad of addictions or criminal behaviors.

In this story, Lauren needs to work through serious abandonment and trust issues that have deeply affected her. It wouldn't be truthful to say that she's figured it all out and all wounds are healed by the end of the story, but she's headed in a healthy direction.

Health and wholeness, my friends, is God's will for each of us—if we will put our trust in Him. The alternative is to become in some fashion like Rolly and Ray (Neil/Marlin).

I pray that you experience God's faithfulness and walk the healing road.

I enjoy hearing from readers so feel free to contact me through my website at www.jillelizabethnelson.com. You can also connect with me on Facebook at facebook.com/JillElizabethNelson.Author.

Abundant Blessings,
Jill Elizabeth Nelson

Get 2 Free Books,
Plus 2 Free Gifts—
just for trying the
Reader Service!

Love Inspired®

Get 2 Free Books,
Plus 2 Free Gifts—
just for trying the Reader Service!

HARLEQUIN
HEARTWARMING™

HOMETOWN HEARTS ♥

YES! Please send me **The Hometown Hearts Collection** in Larger Print. This collection begins with 3 FREE books and 2 FREE gifts in the first shipment. Along with my 3 free books, I'll also get the next 4 books from the Hometown Hearts Collection, in LARGER PRINT, which I may either return and owe nothing, or keep for the low price of $4.99 U.S./ $5.89 CDN each plus $2.99 for shipping and handling per shipment*. If I decide to continue, about once a month for 8 months I will get 6 or 7 more books, but will only need to pay for 4. That means 2 or 3 books in every shipment will be FREE! If I decide to keep the entire collection, I'll have paid for only 32 books because 19 books are FREE! I understand that accepting the 3 free books and gifts places me under no obligation to buy anything. I can always return a shipment and cancel at any time. My free books and gifts are mine to keep no matter what I decide.

262 HCN 3432 462 HCN 3432

Name _____ (PLEASE PRINT) _____

Address _____ Apt. # _____

City _____ State/Prov. _____ Zip/Postal Code _____

Signature (if under 18, a parent or guardian must sign)

Mail to the **Reader Service:**

IN U.S.A.: P.O. Box 1867, Buffalo, NY. 14240-1867
IN CANADA: P.O. Box 609, Fort Erie, Ontario L2A 5X3

READERSERVICE.COM

Manage your account online!

- Review your order history
- Manage your payments
- Update your address

> *We've designed the*
> *Reader Service website*
> *just for you.*

Enjoy all the features!

- Discover new series available to you, and read excerpts from any series.
- Respond to mailings and special monthly offers.
- Browse the Bonus Bucks catalog and online-only exculsives.
- Share your feedback.

Visit us at:
ReaderService.com

RS16R